Dear Readers,

We're so excited to release  Bros. 47 R.O.N.I.N.! When book series, we wanted to create stories kids our age would love. So we jam-packed our series with all of the cool things we love to read about—top secret plots, ninja fighters, ancient samurai weapons, and ultimate villains. We even have a lot in common with the main characters, Tom and Mitch, from our favorite desserts to our favorite bands. Because we love comics so much, we've included original comic book-style art—illustrated by an awesome comic book artist—in each book. We think it rocks, and we hope you do too!

Thanks for reading our series, and stay tuned for future episodes of Sprouse Bros. 47 R.O.N.I.N.!

Dylan Sprouse and Cole Sprouse

We would like to thank our dad and our manager, Josh, for their constant support. Thanks also to everyone at Dualstar and Simon & Schuster for all of their hard work. Last, but not least, thanks to all of our friends and fans—this is for you guys!
—Dylan Sprouse and Cole Sprouse

SIMON SPOTLIGHT

An imprint of Simon & Schuster Children's Publishing Division • 1230 Avenue of the Americas, New York, New York 10020

Sprouse Bros.™ and related *Sprouse Bros.* trademarks are trademarks of DC Sprouse Inc. and licensed exclusively by Dualstar Entertainment Group, LLC. © 2007. DC Sprouse, Inc. All rights reserved, including the right of reproduction in whole or in part in any form.

SIMON SPOTLIGHT and colophon are registered trademarks of Simon & Schuster, Inc.

Manufactured in the United States of America • First Edition   10 9 8 7 6 5 4 3 2 1

ISBN-13: 978-1-4169-3607-7 • ISBN-10: 1-4169-3607-6

Library of Congress Catalog Card Number 2007923464

47 r·o·n·i·n

EPISODE 1 THE REVELATION

by Marc Cerasini
with Dylan Sprouse and Cole Sprouse
based on the series concept created by Marc Cerasini
with Dylan Sprouse and Cole Sprouse
illustrated by Lawrence Christmas

Simon Spotlight
New York London Toronto Sydney

Beginning is easy. Continuing is hard.
—*Japanese proverb*

PROLOGUE

To passing fishermen, the remote Pacific island appeared deserted. Its single barren mountain displayed no trees or fresh water. No animals lived there, not even birds roosted among its jagged cliffs. Only the dragon seemed alive, and only at night, when its eyes glowed green in the tomb-black darkness.

The dragon sat high above the sea. Its wingless form was carved from the rarest jade. Its eyes were fashioned from emeralds larger than ripe green apples. Ripping winds howled around the jade dragon and dangerous waves crashed far below it, yet the dragon's serene expression had been sculpted to convey a feeling of dedicated transcendence—an unshakable calm that knows no fear.

Behind the dragon stood a hidden cave. For more than four hundred years, its yawning mouth remained free of gates or barriers, yet few human beings knew of its existence or dared to venture beyond the statue guarding its entrance.

Torches lined the rock passage, which reached deep into the cliffs. At the end of the craggy corridor, a large chamber opened up. Here the rough walls became strangely smooth. The dirt floor turned into a single solid slab of polished green jade.

Carved into the floor were intricate images: a wolf, a falcon, a tiger, a monkey. There were forty-seven emblems in all, placed in a vast circle around the floor's edge.

In the middle of the chamber, a suit of samurai armor hung. The armor was dented and old. Like the jade dragon at the mouth of the cave, it appeared to serve as some kind of guardian—an eternal sentry.

Outside, the night sky was calm. Out of the stillness came the sound of stone grinding against stone. A hidden door slid open in the cave's rock wall.

A man stepped into the flickering light. A mask of green silk loosely covering his nose and mouth became visible as he emerged from the dark doorway. . . .

CHAPTER 1

The sliding doors opened and the crowd poured into the subway train. Tom and Mitch Hearn flowed along with the pushing, shoving mass.

At fifteen, the twin brothers were wiry enough to squeeze through the horde. They squirmed all the way to the end of the last car. Every seat was taken—no surprise—so they stood.

Tom shook his head. "You just *had* to go to the computer store after school, didn't you?"

Mitch blinked. "Excuse me? I had an inspiration during study hall, and I had to act on it. Your point?"

"It's after four." Tom tapped his wristwatch and gestured to the crush of bodies. "You're the reason we're stuck in the middle of rush hour."

Mitch rolled his eyes. "Right, Pokey, like you didn't spend the entire time playing that new video game at the demonstration booth?"

"Listen, Motormouth, it was either that or listen to you talk gigabytes with the Geek Squad."

The doors closed and the train pulled away from the underground station. The brothers gazed out the back window, watching the concrete platform recede. When the tunnel's darkness swallowed the last bit of fluorescent light, Tom shifted his overstuffed and cumbersome backpack onto his shoulder. He unzipped his sweatshirt and pulled back his hood.

As twins, Tom and Mitch shared many features—fair complexions, blue eyes, even a scattering of freckles across their noses. The two wore their straw-colored hair in shaggy mops long enough to touch their collars. But the boys were far from exact duplicates.

Tom was a bit more built up than his brother, a by-product of his interest in sports and martial arts. Mitch attended the same martial arts classes, but found tech stuff a lot more interesting than kicking and punching drills.

"I told you I had an inspiration," Mitch reminded his brother. "I needed a new digital processor to power-boost my science project." He tightened his grip on the silver pole. "I'm going to win the Citywide Science Fair this year, even if it *kills* me."

"Dude!" Tom replied, feigning alarm. "Just because that girl from Chinatown beat the living daylights out of you doesn't mean you should throw your life away."

Mitch smirked. "Her miniature microwave transmitter threw half the city's FM radio stations off-line."

Tom laughed. "She won, didn't she?"

"If you ask me, she was a walking disaster area!" Mitch threw his arms wide and accidentally bumped a woman's overstuffed shopping bag. The woman gave him a nasty look. Mitch didn't notice. "She should have been reported to the Federal Communications Commission!"

"Well, she wasn't," Tom said. "She won the first place trophy, which pretty much makes her Princess Nerd. Soon *she'll* be working for the Geek Squad."

"The Citywide Science Fair trophy is hotly coveted, bro. And this year it's coming home with *me*." Mitch scratched an itch behind his ear and touched something small and hard tangled in his shaggy blond hair. He carefully extracted the object.

"My micro-motherboard!" He displayed the tiny silicon chip. "I was looking all over for this little sucker!"

Tom sighed in disgust. "You are such a dork. Sometimes I can't believe we're related. Next you'll be wearing extra-thick glasses and carrying a pocket protector."

"I don't need glasses. But carrying a pocket protector is actually a good idea," Mitch noted. "Last month I forgot to cap one of my felt-tips. Totally ruined my Teriyaki Boyz T-shirt."

"Uncool, dude," Tom replied. "I mean it, man. Seriously uncool. Don't even joke about stuff like that. Maybe you don't care, but I have a reputation to uphold."

Mitch rolled his eyes. "Relax, bro, I'm not *that* nerdy."

"That's debatable."

"Anyway," Mitch continued, slipping the chip into a pocket of his backpack, "cool is totally subjective. To some, it's wearing a Kangol cap and listening to an iPod. To me, it's winning the Citywide Science Fair trophy, which will, *no doubt*, lead to early graduation, acceptance by an Ivy League college, and a subsequent path to wealth, fame, and legions of hotties with brains."

"Your point?" Tom demanded.

"To you, cool is apparently the absence of a pocket protector, and cutting history class to skateboard in the alley behind the school—which, by the way, could lead to expulsion, juvenile delinquency, and be followed by a life of crime. At best you'll end up with a full-time career flipping hamburgers, but only after you've made early parole at a state-run correction facility. . . ."

Mitch stopped talking when he realized Tom was no longer paying attention. His brother had gone back to staring out the rear window of the subway train. But there was nothing to see. No work crew to gawk at. Not even a passing train on a parallel track—just the tunnel behind them, stretching into endless darkness.

"Ground control to Major Tom," Mitch called.

Tom blinked. "Sorry. Guess I zoned out. You were saying something about me cutting history class?"

"Selective hearing," said Mitch. "That must be so nice for you. The bad news is that I tried to cover for you with Mr. Giordano, but he wasn't buying what I was selling. He said you—"

Tom cut his brother off. "Giordano caught me at my locker when I came back for my stuff at the end of the day."

"How bad did you get hit?" Mitch asked.

"Five pages on the ramifications of Columbus's discovery of the New World. Due Monday, nine a.m."

Mitch winced sympathetically. "Ouch! Is skate-boarding really worth the extra homework?"

"Absolutely," Tom replied. "It's only the end of October. I've still got to wait at least six weeks for snowboarding season to start. And how's my ditching history any different from you ducking workouts at the dojo to play on your computer, anyway?"

"I'm not playing," Mitch protested. "I'm *inventing*."

"Dude, so was I! I mastered the back stair rail. Rode top to bottom and made a soft landing—twice in a row. It was *so* Tony Hawk!" Tom paused a moment and stroked his chin, pretending to be lost in thought. "You know, Mitch, now that I think about it, you're right."

"I'm right?" Mitch's eyes widened. "Wait. I should pull out my cell phone to capture this moment digitally. Dad'll never believe it."

"No, really, it's my mistake," Tom insisted. "You *don't* do much dodging at the dojo. Since your head's always in cyberspace, just about anyone can *hit* you."

"You are so dead." Mitch feigned a blow to his brother's chin, then a soft undercut to his gut. "Ha! Sucker! You know I'm just as good as you are. Besides, you pick up those weird moves of yours watching

Samurai Wind, not at the dojo. The sensei would not approve."

Tom glanced at his watch again. "Speaking of . . . we're never going to get home in time to see today's episode if this train doesn't pick up speed. They might reveal the identity of the Black Ninja!"

"That'll never happen," Mitch said. "Anyway, I set the DVR before we left for school this morning."

"Excellent!" Tom smiled. "You know, you're not a bad *little* brother, for a complete dork."

"You had fifteen minutes of fame, bro. Then I arrived and your time was up. Get over yourself."

Tom and Mitch rode together in silence for a few minutes. Then Mitch noticed the zoned-out expression on Tom's troubled face. He could tell his brother was buggin' about something. And he knew his twin well enough to know what was eating him.

"Still freaking over that dream you had last night?" Mitch asked.

"Yeah." Tom shrugged. "It was just so . . . real. The mountain. The cave. It's like it was all happening somewhere, and I was watching it."

"If it's really bothering you, talk to Dad about it when he gets home," Mitch suggested.

Tom's expression darkened. "The operative word is *when*. As in *when* might that be?"

Now Mitch frowned. Jack Hearn's unexplained absence was the ugly subject they'd both avoided acknowledging. But now that the leopard was out of the bag, as their father often said, there was no use pretending it might not bite them.

"Dad should have been back a week ago. But he hasn't even called since last Friday. Business must be keeping him *extraordinarily* busy." Tom's tone was skeptical.

"Actually," Mitch admitted, "this morning I asked Mr. Chance when Dad was coming back."

"What did he say?"

Mitch shrugged. "He got all weird on me. Shooed me out of the kitchen."

"The Chance Man is *always* weird," Tom replied. "But I know what you mean. He did that to me two days ago when I asked. It's like he's trying to dodge the question instead of answering it."

"There's more." Mitch's frown deepened. "Last night after you went to bed, I snuck into Dad's office, bypassed his security system, and hacked into his computer—"

"Dude!" cried Tom. "He's gonna waste you!"

"I checked Dad's ISP account—"

Tom didn't like the troubled look on his brother's face. "And?"

"Dad hasn't signed on for six days—hasn't even opened his e-mails in almost a week."

Now Tom was troubled too. Their father hadn't phoned or even sent an e-mail in over a week.

Tom tapped his brother's shoulder and pointed to the window. "This is our stop."

The doors opened, but getting off the train during rush hour was no easy feat. Adults were packed shoulder to shoulder carrying shopping bags, briefcases, and rolling suitcases.

The boys crouched and shoved and squeezed between the big bodies.

"Coming through! Coming through!" Tom called, pushing his brother in front of him until they finally stumbled onto the platform—and just in time. With a swish, the subway car doors closed behind them.

"See what I mean about rush hour?" Tom griped as the train pulled out with an earsplitting rumble.

"Man!" Mitch shouted over the noise. "That dude near the door mashed my instep!"

Tom clutched his ears. "Quit your whining, baby."

"Sorry, but there's no other way to clear ninety-five decibels!" Mitch shook his head. "The MTA really should get some rubber insulation on those steel wheels!"

As the deafening roar dissipated into the dark tunnel, the boys started walking. They'd been riding in the very last subway car, so it was a long way to the exit. Most of the passengers were in front of them, rushing down the long platform, toward the stairs and the fading autumn daylight.

As the boys followed behind the crowd, a lone figure stepped right into their path. The man's appearance surprised them. He was clad in dark, skintight clothing from the top of his hooded head to his split-toed boots. On his belt the stranger wore a traditional samurai sword, contained in an ornate scabbard.

Tom blinked in amazement. "Wow! What an awesome Halloween costume! You look just like the Black Ninja from . . ."

Tom's voice trailed off when he saw the stranger drop into a fighting stance.

"No need to freak out, man," Mitch said, trying to end any confrontation before things escalated. "We were just admiring the costume."

The man looked at Mitch through a slit in his hood. Though it seemed from his positioning that the ninja was going to attack, he just stood there, silently. Then, for a split second, Mitch thought the ninja was going to say something when suddenly a loud clanking sound echoed from the other side of the tracks. With a whisper of steel against steel, he slid the sword free of its scabbard and raised it above his head, until the silver blade glimmered under the subway station's fluorescent lights.

The black-clad ninja looked around, as if making sure that they were alone on the platform. Across the way on the downtown track, he spotted a darkened figure hiding in the corner. Then, without uttering a sound, the ninja attacked.

CHAPTER 2

"I don't think this guy's going to the Village Halloween parade," Tom murmured.

As the ninja lunged toward Mitch, Tom grabbed his paralyzed brother and yanked him out of the way. Just in time, too. The sword sliced through the spot where Mitch's head had been a second before.

Tom searched for a way out. Behind them was a solid wall. In front of them was the ninja. The train was already gone, so they couldn't jump back on it. And the ten-foot drop off the platform edge would only take them down to the electrified subway tracks.

The ninja had planned his attack well. He had them cornered on the narrow strip of concrete, and there wasn't a police officer in sight.

Seriously not good, Tom decided.

The sword cut the air again. Instinctively drawing on their martial arts training, Tom and Mitch both dropped to the floor as the blade whistled over their heads.

While Mitch rolled under a large wooden bench, Tom jumped to his feet again, poised for a counterattack.

"Aiiiiii-YAH!"

Tom's howl was accompanied by a reverse-left high straight kick. Though he was working toward his brown belt, the maneuver was complex and difficult, and he couldn't quite pull it off.

The ninja's dodge was lightning fast, and Tom's foot connected with nothing but empty air.

Not expecting to miss—and not balanced enough to recover—Tom landed hard on the concrete. Momentarily stunned, he watched the ninja raise his sword over him. As it came down, he felt hands yanking on the straps of his backpack.

"Over here!" Mitch grunted, dragging his brother under the bench. "Man, you usually spar way better than *that*!" he added.

"He took me by surprise, that's all," Tom shot back. "Don't panic. If we work together, we can take this punk down."

The ninja's sword struck sparks off the concrete. The assassin whirled around and spied the brothers under the cover of a wooden seat. Muffled by the mask, the ninja sounded like he was trying to speak. He had them cornered. Once more he looked across the downtown platform, then turned back around to face the boys, and, raising his sword, the assassin prepared to cut right through the bench to strike them down.

Tom whispered a curse in frustration.

Mitch gritted his teeth. "Where's Jet Li when you need him?"

The ninja chuckled.

Just then, a bystander rushed forward. In a few quick, powerful leaps, the stranger landed on top of the bench and dropped into a classic fighting crouch, seemingly unafraid to square off against the ninja.

Peeking out from below, the boys couldn't see the stranger's face. But they saw enough of the dude to wonder about his sanity. The skinny kid was no bigger than they were, which meant he was half the size of the ninja. He wore a hooded gym suit. His wool cap doubled as a ski mask, and it was now pulled all the way down, covering his entire face.

The ninja's eyes glinted when he faced his small foe. Suddenly the stranger expertly delivered an elbow hook to the assassin's chin.

The blow came from the ninja's blind side and staggered him. Still moving, the newcomer seized the blade with all of his might. With a quick twist, the sword was wrenched from the assassin's grip and clattered across the dirty subway platform.

"Whoa," Mitch murmured, "maybe we *don't* need Jet Li."

"This kid's amazing!" Tom cried.

The brothers rolled out from under the bench—too soon, as it turned out. The ninja stepped back and reached into his black clothes. In a quick motion, he drew two shiny metal shuriken, hurling them both at the same time.

"Incoming!" Mitch ducked and the razor-sharp throwing star gouged chips off the tiled wall above his head.

Tom twisted his body; he felt a jolt. Just missing his torso, the shuriken had embedded itself in his bulky backpack.

Mitch's eyes widened. "Saved by a history assignment!"

While the ninja was occupied, the stranger stepped in from his blind side and shot a straight right jab to his jaw, followed by a hard straight left. Though the little masked fighter wasn't strong enough to bring the assassin down, the traditional one-two punch *did* rock the ninja's world.

Sensing an advantage, the masked stranger didn't let up, delivering another one-two combination, followed by a series of jabs and hand strikes to the ninja's body.

Finally the stranger danced on the balls of his feet and delivered a high straight kick with his left foot.

Tom watched in amazement. "Who is this dude?"

Mitch shook his head. "I don't know, but maybe we should help him."

Before Tom could reply, Mitch struck. His attack was fast, but clumsy. The ninja saw him coming and easily countered the blow. Instead of connecting with the assassin, Mitch was tossed into the stranger, sending them both to the concrete.

"Sorry!" Mitch moaned.

A hollow tinkling sounded as the stranger rolled over. Mitch noticed a small blue object on the concrete. It had fallen from the kid's coat pocket.

"Dude? Are you okay?" Mitch asked.

The stranger didn't reply. He was too busy pulling at his hair. He'd obviously stuffed it beneath his loose jacket. Now that it was partially out, he pulled it completely free. Mitch was surprised to see how long it was. The black ponytail streamed all the way down the stranger's back.

By now the ninja had retrieved his sword and was charging them both.

"We need to work together," Mitch told the small fighter. "It's our only chance."

The stranger nodded and crouched into a ready

stance, hands raised. Suddenly another battle cry echoed inside the subway station.

Tom was charging again, and this time he was airborne. His flying leap kick connected with the ninja's skull. Grunting, the assassin dropped to his knees.

Tom landed in front of him—on his *feet* this time. Legs braced, fists raised, he asked the ninja, "Give up yet?"

The assassin replied by dropping onto his back and kicking out with both legs. Fortunately for Tom, the ninja's drop kick missed him by an inch. The four fighters stood in silence for a split second.

"This is the police!" a voice boomed suddenly.

Tom rolled off Mitch and looked up. Three NYPD police officers hurried across the subway platform.

"Put your hands in front of you and get down on the ground!" one officer commanded, gun drawn.

The ninja ignored the cop. He shot a final look at the boys. Then he retrieved his sword and leaped off the station's platform onto the tracks. As the roar of an approaching train battered their ears, Mitch and Tom watched as the ninja raced into the tunnel, his black clothing melting into the darkness.

To the brothers' surprise, the police continued their pursuit. They commanded the assassin to halt in the name of the law. But the ninja just kept going. The cops followed him into the blackness.

The train rolled into the station, but it didn't leave. Evidently, the police had just officially frozen all traffic along this stretch of the subway. The manhunt for the ninja was going to mess up rush hour, big-time.

On the platform, Tom rose to his feet and dusted himself off. Mitch ran a shaky hand through his shaggy blond hair.

"What's that guy's problem, anyway?" Tom asked. "We didn't do anything to him!"

Mitch shrugged. "I don't know. But if it wasn't for the dude with the ski mask, we'd have been chopped into little pieces."

Tom turned to face the stranger. "Thanks for the help. We—"

But the stranger was gone.

"Did you get a good look at him?" Mitch asked.

"Sorry," said Tom. "My X-ray vision is on the fritz again. He was wearing a ski mask, remember?"

Mitch noticed a blue spot of color on the ground. He bent down and picked up a small object.

"What's that?" Tom asked.

"It fell out of the stranger's pocket," Mitch replied, examining the small plastic object. "Looks like a cap for a computer thumb drive."

Tom examined it. "TM," he read, running his thumb

over the white letters etched into the blue cap.

"You know, it's weird," Mitch said, taking the cap back. "I can't place him, but there was something familiar about that dude."

"You know anybody with the initials TM?" Tom asked.

Mitch shook his head. "No."

Tom snorted. "I don't suppose you've met our friendly ninja assassin before too."

Mitch yanked the shuriken out of his brother's backpack, hefting it in his hand.

"I think I would have remembered him," he quipped. "A guy like that leaves quite an impression."

CHAPTER 3

Mitch and Tom fidgeted at the dining-room table, still buzzed from the incident in the subway. The throwing star that had pierced Tom's backpack, and the blue thumb-drive cap displaying the letters TM, lay side by side on the white tablecloth between them.

There wasn't much interesting about the cap. Mitch figured the TM could just stand for "trademark" anyway, and that didn't tell them much. The finely crafted shuriken was another matter. The boys examined the amazing weapon, careful not to get nicked by the tapered blades. Roughly the size of one of their hands, the metal star had six points and an enameled design in the center.

"If he was a ninja, what was he doing attacking us on a subway platform during rush hour?" Tom asked. "I thought ninjas wore black and struck only at night."

"Not true, actually," Mitch replied. "Historically,

ninjas dressed to blend in with their surroundings, including the people around them. Then they would strike, and fade back into the scenery."

Tom nodded. "Guess that explains why he wore black. The subway tunnel was going to be his escape route from the start."

"Right," Mitch replied. "And we were attacked on the subway because if the ninja waited until nighttime to attack us, he'd have to break into the house."

Tom laughed. "You got that right. With the Chance Man in charge, we're never out at night!"

The kitchen door opened, and the brothers looked up guiltily. Mr. Chance entered the dining room, a covered tray in his hands.

"Your first course," he announced in a solemn tone.

A compact Japanese man with stone gray hair, Mr. Chance was a wiry bundle of dynamic energy. He was always ready with their breakfast when they woke, and he was constantly tinkering around the house for hours after they went to bed. Mitch and Tom sometimes wondered whether the man slept at all. No matter the hour, Mr. Chance always seemed to be awake and alert.

Today, as always, he wore his uniform: a suit over a collarless shirt. The man's conduct was as formal as his attire. He'd been the family cook and butler since Tom and Mitch were seven years old. When their mom died,

Tom and Mitch needed looking after. Jack was always away on business, so he hired Mr. Chance to hold down the fort. After eight years of loyal servitude, Mr. Chance was considered part of the family.

Mr. Chance set the tray on the table between them and lifted the lid off a tureen of soup. "The soup du jour is vegetarian vegetable," he declared amid a cloud of steam.

"How can you serve soup at a time like this?" Mitch asked.

Mr. Chance stared. "Why, a chilly autumn evening is the *perfect* time to serve soup. It warms the innards."

"Weren't you listening?" Tom demanded. "We were telling you about the ninja on the subway."

"Of course I was listening," Mr. Chance replied. "I'm listening still." He meticulously ladled soup into the center of each bowl. Not a drop was spilled or splattered. "You have endlessly recounted the plot of your favorite samurai cartoon since you returned from school this afternoon. And you were *late*, I might add."

Mitch closed his eyes and shook his head. "We were *late* because of the *attack*. We told you already."

Mr. Chance wagged his finger disapprovingly. "You should have informed me you were going to a friend's house to watch *The Breezy Samurai*—"

"That's *Samurai Wind*," Tom corrected, drumming his

fingers on the table. "And that's not what happened."

"In any case," Mr. Chance continued, "I expected you home promptly at four thirty p.m. But you didn't arrive until nearly six thirty."

"That's because *the ninja attacked us*, right on the *subway platform*," Tom repeated in exasperation.

Mr. Chance leveled his gaze at Tom. "I am sure your father would praise your vivid imagination, young man. However, your argumentative exaggerations impress me even less than the fact that you cut history class."

"You . . . uh, you know about that?" Tom asked.

Mr. Chance passed Mitch a basket filled with bread sticks. "I received a phone call from Mr. Giordano this afternoon. He takes a rather dim view of your absence."

"Okay, my bad," Tom admitted. "But forget history. This time it isn't an excuse. We're telling the truth about the ninja." He snatched the shuriken off the table and waved it under Mr. Chance's nose. "Here's the proof!"

Mr. Chance hardly glanced at the metal star. "Did you purchase that in a souvenir shop?" he asked with only mild curiosity. "Not a wise use of your allowance, young sir. But I suppose it's your money to spend."

"I didn't *buy* this at a shop," Tom insisted. "The guy who attacked us threw it at me."

Mr. Chance stared at the object in silence. "That's not a toy, and it's certainly much too dangerous to be tossed about. Perhaps you should hand it over to me," Mr. Chance suggested.

Mitch leaped up and grabbed it from his brother. "Not until I study it closer. There's a design engraved on one side. See . . ." He pointed. "It's some kind of black flower."

"It is a lotus blossom," Mr. Chance informed them, covering the soup tureen. "The genus *Lotus*, from the subfamily Faboideae, in the family Fabaceae. Most common is the European lotus flower, which is white. The Egyptian blossom is either white or blue. Asian flowers are generally fiery orange, yellow, or red."

Mr. Chance paused and a strange expression crossed his face. "I am not familiar with a *black* lotus, however."

The brothers stared at their butler. "How do you know all that?" asked Mitch.

The man's lips lifted in a slight smile. "Before I entered your father's service, I arranged flowers in a florist's shop."

Tom seemed skeptical. "I thought you said you were a cook in a Japanese restaurant."

"Huh?" Mitch said. "Mr. Chance told *me* he was a merchant marine aboard a tramp steamer out of Hong Kong."

The brothers fixed their gazes on Mr. Chance, waiting for an explanation.

"A person can travel many paths in his lifetime," the butler explained. Then he gestured to the steaming bowls. "Now eat your soup before it gets cold. I shall serve the buckwheat noodles next. And Tom, you will be delighted to learn that I have prepared tapioca pudding for dessert."

"Nice. How 'bout we skip the noodles, then," Tom suggested.

Mr. Chance ignored him. "And after dessert—*homework*."

The brothers moaned. "But it's *Friday*," Tom protested. "We have all weekend to finish our work."

"True," Mitch agreed. "I planned on watching some—"

"No television," Mr. Chance announced. "Seems to me you've both had enough violent entertainment for one day. Now, I must excuse myself for a moment to make a phone call. When I return, I expect to see those bowls empty."

侍

"Finished!" Tom boasted, closing his laptop. "I've written five—count 'em, *five*—gripping and factual pages on the ramifications of Christopher Columbus's discovery of the New World."

"Congratulations, Pokey, Mr. Giordano will be thrilled." Mitch glanced at his watch. "I had two papers to write, and I was done an hour ago."

Since he'd already completed his assignments, Mitch had been gazing at the lights of the United Nations building not far away. From their bedroom window on the third floor, they could also see the East River.

Giant black barges and brightly lit pleasure yachts drifted on the dark waterway. Across the river, a huge red Coca-Cola logo marked the opposite shoreline in the borough of Queens.

Tom yawned and stretched. "It's not even nine o'clock, and it's T.G.I.F. What do we do now?"

"Mr. Chance has decreed television off-limits, so why don't we go hang out in my workshop?" Mitch said.

"And watch you slap circuits together?" A look of revulsion crossed Tom's face. "I'd rather go to bed."

Just then the phone rang. "I'll get it, young sirs," Mr. Chance announced. "It's just someone from my new cooking class."

"Mr. Chance is taking a cooking class?" Tom asked.

Uninterested, Mitch changed the subject.

"Do me a favor. Let me use your laptop. You can use

my big computer downstairs," Mitch offered.

"Why would I want to use your desktop?"

"Because last night when you were sleeping I downloaded Samurai Wind Challenge for PC."

Tom jumped out of his chair. "Game on!"

With the shuriken in his hand and his brother's laptop under his arm, Mitch headed downstairs. Tom happily followed.

The brothers lived in a three-story brownstone on the east side of Manhattan. Mr. Chance had his own apartment below theirs, on the second floor, right next to their father's home office. Both were empty at the moment.

The boys descended all the way down to the first floor, past the living room, dining room, guest room, and a study filled with books. They could hear Mr. Chance tinkering in the kitchen.

After a final flight of stairs, they arrived at the basement garage. The walls were exposed, showing off the century-old red brick. Pipes hung over their heads. Two street-level windows near the ceiling looked out on an alley behind the building.

Mitch's workshop dominated one side of the garage. Their father's black Hummer and Mr. Chance's silver PT Cruiser occupied the opposite end, directly under the windows. An automatic garage door opened to a ramp that flowed onto a side street near the corner of Manhattan's busy First Avenue.

Mitch powered up the desktop computer and then replaced the keyboard with a game controller. In a moment the introduction to the Samurai Wind Challenge video game was displayed on the high-definition screen. Tom sat down behind the desk and was soon battling cyberfoes.

Meanwhile, Mitch slumped down at his workbench amid a treasure trove of old toys, new tools, partially assembled electronic gadgets, bits and pieces of disassembled computers, MP3 players, and a digital recorder. The throwing star next to him, he powered up his brother's laptop. In a moment he was surfing the Web for information about the black lotus.

"I wonder why Mr. Chance doesn't believe we were attacked," Mitch said after long minutes of silent searching.

Tom twisted the joystick to dispatch a foe. "Well, you have to admit it sounds kind of crazy. . . ."

"It's not *that* crazy," Mitch argued. "This is New York City."

"Ha, ha," said Tom, not amused. "And maybe our ninja was just an old-fashioned New York City nutcase. This burg is full of them."

"Well, if you want to know the truth, I blame you for

Mr. Chance's attitude," Mitch said.

"*Me?*" Tom cried, looking at his brother in shock. Then his eyes quickly darted back to the game.

"Sure. Why should Mr. Chance believe us after he gets a call from Mr. Giordano? It makes this whole ninja story sound like another one of your whoppers."

"But we have *proof*," Tom insisted. "The shuriken . . ."

Mitch shook his head. "It's not good enough for Mr. Chance. Dad would believe us, though, if he were here. And he wouldn't need proof."

Tom hit the game's pause button and spun the chair to face his brother. That's when they heard the noise.

"What's that?" Mitch hissed.

"Shh," Tom whispered. "It's coming from over there, between the two cars. . . ."

They listened again. The noise sounded like stone rubbing against stone. Strangely, it seemed to be coming from *behind* the solid brick wall.

While Mitch and Tom stared in shock, a door opened where no door had existed before. Then came an even bigger shock—a ninja in a black battle suit and split-toed boots stepped over the threshold, his sword drawn.

CHAPTER 4

The masked intruder gripped the long silver blade with both hands and raised the sword over his head. Without a sound, he rushed them.

Tom rolled off his chair, then shoved it into the path of their attacker. Rumbling on uneven wheels, the chair careened into the narrow space between the two cars, bumping to a halt against the Hummer.

Effortlessly, the ninja leaped over the barrier, sword flashing under the stark fluorescent lights.

Mitch grabbed Tom's laptop and raised it above his head as a shield—just in time. The blade descended, slicing the computer in half. Letter keys, microchips, and components rained down on Mitch like plastic confetti.

The ninja growled and wheeled to strike again.

But he never got the chance.

Protecting his brother, Tom threw himself between

Mitch and the ninja. Crouching low, Tom spun, sweeping the man's legs out from under him. The ninja flew backward, body-slamming the workbench.

Before the ninja could rise, Tom lunged with a side kick that pinned the man's wrist against the bench. The weapon dropped out of the ninja's twitching hand. Mitch rushed forward and soccer-kicked the blade under the Hummer.

Recovering quickly, the ninja deflected Tom's straight kick. Dancing away, Tom balanced on the balls of his feet, eyes glued to his foe. Fists raised, he continued to shield his brother.

The ninja spied the throwing star on the bench and snapped it up. He raised the shuriken and tossed it in one fluid motion. Before Tom or Mitch could react, a silver streak shot over their heads.

The kitchen knife struck the throwing star in midair. The knife shattered. Deflected, the shuriken struck sparks off the brick wall and bounced harmlessly into a corner.

"Get behind me, young sirs," Mr. Chance said.

The butler stepped between the brothers and the ninja. Mr. Chance still wore an apron, his sleeves rolled up. He'd been cleaning, and dishwashing soap still clung to his forearms.

There was no face-off. No dramatic moment where

the rivals took measure of each other. Mr. Chance simply struck, fast as lightning and full of fury—like some tiny package of dynamite that finally exploded.

Whirling, kicking, ducking, and punching, their beloved butler and cook displayed a martial arts skill Mitch and Tom never imagined he possessed. It took only a few seconds for Mr. Chance's furious assault to force the intruder into a corner. The ninja could barely fend off the continual rain of jabs, hooks, one-two combinations, and straight-out punches.

In desperation, the assassin snatched a piece of the laptop off the workbench and hurled it. Mr. Chance ducked, and the machine shattered against the wall. More debris showered down on Tom and Mitch.

The unexpected move was enough to throw Mr. Chance off balance, but instead of pressing his momentary advantage, the ninja dropped to the concrete floor and rolled under the Hummer.

"He's going for the sword!" Tom warned.

The ninja popped up on the other side of the car, sheathed his sword, and glared at Mr. Chance with silent menace. Meanwhile, Mr. Chance braced himself for another attack.

But the ninja's next move surprised even Mr. Chance. The black-clad attacker turned and jumped onto the high basement window ledge. In a shower of breaking glass, he squirmed through the tiny opening and melted into the darkness of the alley.

"We've got to do something!" Mitch yelled. "Call the police. Have that guy arrested!"

To their surprise, Mr. Chance shook his head. "The police would never catch him. And if they did, they could not keep him. He is a Black Lotus warrior. No prison cell could hold him for long. His secret allies would soon free him."

Tom's expression was incredulous. "How do you know this?" he cried. "Why did that guy attack us on the subway and then break into our house? Why was he here? What was he looking for?"

Meanwhile, Mitch stared silently at the secret door, its threshold veiled in darkness. "I don't think it was the same guy from the subway. This ninja was way more skilled. Either way, these Black Lotus guys are after us or something we have. Maybe we'll find out what if we go in there—"

Mitch moved forward, but Mr. Chance stopped him with a hand on his shoulder.

"I cannot prevent either of you from going in, but be warned." Mr. Chance's dark eyes rested first on Mitch, then on Tom. "Once you walk through that door, your lives will never again be the same."

Mitch and Tom exchanged glances, then stared at

the doorway. Although Mitch burned with curiosity, he felt paralyzed. For a long minute, he refused to move.

Tom exhaled and shrugged. "You know, Mitch," he said quietly, "with ninjas attacking us in the subway, and intruders popping out of the walls of our garage, I'd say our lives have already changed—and not for the better."

Mitch folded his arms. "Your point?"

Tom locked eyes with his brother. "I'm going through."

Mitch watched his brother stride boldly over the threshold and into the shadows.

For a full minute, Mitch chewed his bottom lip, his mind churning. He still didn't want to go, but because his brother was so impulsive, he had no choice.

After all, he thought, finally stepping forward, somebody's got to watch my brother's back!

CHAPTER 5

Across the shadowy threshold, Mitch found a dark, narrow corridor with a flight of stone stairs descending into absolute gloom.

There was no sign of Tom.

The staircase was made of carved granite blocks, uneven and worn by age. The walls and ceiling were constructed of sandstone that was now crumbling. A heavy dampness caused dust to cling to the rock like delicate icicles. Echoing from somewhere below, Mitch heard the sound of rushing water.

Cautiously, he began his descent. Mitch realized that this tunnel and the stone staircase were much older than the brownstone built over them. So they had to be well over 130 years old, because their father had once told them that their house was constructed in 1872.

With each step, Mitch moved farther into darkness. The silent gloom became oppressive—and scary. There were no railings, so Mitch ran his fingers along the rough stone walls to balance himself.

Finally he reached the bottom of the stairs. Mitch opened his mouth to call his brother's name, when someone grabbed his arm. He whirled and faced a blinding light.

"Hey!" he yelped. "Get that flashlight out of my eyes!"

"Sorry," Tom said. "It's so dark down here, I had to use my Pocket Pal to find my way around."

Tom held the birthday gift from their father: a combination knife, tool kit, and flashlight, wrapped up into a neat package the size of a cell phone.

"Where's yours?" he asked.

Mitch shrugged. "Upstairs. Who knew I'd need survival equipment in my own basement?"

Tom sighed. "That's the *point* of stuff like that, genius. You're supposed to carry it with you at all times, 'cause you never know when disaster will strike." He glanced around at the eerie surroundings. "And in case you haven't noticed, we're not in our own basement anymore."

"So where are we?" Mitch asked, his words echoing hollowly in the stone chamber.

Tom displayed a know-it-all grin. "You've got to see this!"

Using the flashlight beam to probe the blackness, Tom led Mitch along a narrow tunnel. The arched ceiling hung low over their heads, and they frequently had to stoop as they walked along.

The sound of rushing water became a faint roar, like a distant waterfall. They both shivered in the dampness.

"Are we in the sewers?" Mitch wondered aloud.

"Under them, I'd say," Tom replied smugly. For once he'd figured something out before his brother did, and he was feeling pretty proud of himself. He raised the flashlight to illuminate the tunnel ahead. "Check this out. . . ."

Mitch was startled to see that the tunnel ended abruptly, just a few feet in front of them—not at a wall, but at an underground shore. Black water lapped the stones at his feet. Echoing from somewhere in the cave beyond, he heard the sound of rushing water.

"Look at this," Tom said. He shifted the flashlight beam to focus on a bronze plaque embedded in the wall. Mitch read the inscription, written in the sort of flowery printing he'd seen in Colonial-era documents.

"The Sound River?" Mitch said. "I remember that from history class. That's the old name for the East River."

SOUND RIVER

"Mr. Giordano again," Tom grumbled. "He's the bane of my existence."

"Whoa!" cried Mitch. "I think I figured out where our intruder came from. Shine the light over there."

Tom directed the light to the floor near the lapping waters. Illuminated in the flashlight's beam was a shiny black wetsuit, which lay like a puddle on the stone floor. Beside it were a pair of flippers and a snorkeling mask.

Mitch prodded the gear with his foot. "There must be a way in, a tunnel or pipe or something that leads to the East River." He looked at his brother. "I'll bet he was planning to use this tunnel to escape, too," he added.

"That still doesn't explain what the ninja was looking for in the first place. There's nothing down here but a dead end," Tom said, his voice edged with frustration. "And I can't see how finding a tunnel under our house changes my life forever, anyway. Seems like Mr. Chance is making up stories now. . . ."

"Listen!" Mitch seized his brother's arm.

They both heard it—a grinding sound behind them. They spun in time to see a bright white light cutting through the dimness.

"It's another secret door," Mitch whispered. "It opened up at the base of the stairs."

"But we were just there, and I didn't see any door—or even a doorway. Did you?" Tom asked.

Mitch shrugged. "We didn't see the door in our basement, either. Not until it opened up."

"Come on," Tom cried. "Let's go check it out."

Before Mitch could stop him, Tom took off at a run.

"Hey, wait!" cried Mitch. "It might be dangerous! There might be more intruders."

If Tom heard his brother, he paid no attention. Mitch watched the wavering flashlight and heard Tom's feet pounding on the stone floor as he raced down the corridor.

Here we go again, Mitch thought, jogging to catch up to his brother. The only time Tom isn't Pokey is when he ought to be!

CHAPTER 6

Tom stopped short at the open door. After the dim tunnel, he felt blinded by the brilliant light streaming out of the room ahead.

Mitch collided into him and they both lost their balance. Their arms shot out, and they used each other to steady themselves.

When their vision had adjusted, the brothers moved across the threshold. The wall slid back into place behind them, and they found themselves in a massive circular room.

"Whoa," Tom whispered.

"What the . . ." Mitch murmured. It felt to him as if he'd crossed a time barrier. In a few steps they'd left behind a gloomy Colonial-era tunnel and entered a brilliant high-tech future.

Mainframe computers lined the curved stone walls, each with its own monitor and workstation. Suspended above their heads, dozens of digital televisions dangled from the ceiling like a high-definition chandelier.

Many of the screens scrolled columns of letters and numbers. Encrypted data, was Mitch's guess. Other screens displayed grid maps, or geometric shapes that morphed constantly. A few appeared to show real-time satellite imagery that was beamed in directly from space.

But Tom soon discovered that not everything in this chamber was modern. The coolest stuff to him was not cutting edge—more like cutting-*edged*.

A battle-worn suit of medieval armor stood between banks of late-model computers. Mounted on the wall behind it were swords, spears, longbows, and several crossbows. They hung on a heavy, wheel-shaped rack of ancient wood. But the place of honor seemed to be given to the weapon at the center of the display. Against a flat shield of gold hung a three-bladed dagger.

As Tom circled the room, he also found a bundle of long pikes, a rack of straight-handled maces, chain maces, hatchets, and even a two-handed ax.

"Right, this makes sense," he murmured sarcastically.

It wasn't long before Tom realized that not a single one of the weapons inside this chamber was modern. There were no guns or rifles. No firearms of any kind, only traditional melee weapons used in face-to-face, one-on-one combat.

Mitch hadn't noticed what his brother was doing. His gaze had been fixed on the high-definition monitors, his mind racing as he tried to make sense of the megabits of data dancing across the screens.

Tom was suddenly transfixed too—but not by the screens. He'd caught sight of a large banner suspended from the ceiling. In the center of a white background was a beautiful wingless dragon.

Apart from the style of the picture, Tom knew the dragon was Asian because of Mr. Chance. Years before, he'd read them a bedtime story about a dragon. He'd mentioned in passing that Asian cultures believed dragons needed no wings because they could fly by magic. Tom never forgot that.

This dragon image was mesmerizing. The creature was jade green with emerald eyes. Although it looked fierce, its expression gave the feeling of peace and transcendence. It also looked strangely familiar.

"I've seen this dragon," Tom whispered. It was the exact dragon from his bizarre dream about the mysterious island and the hidden cave.

He moved closer to the banner and noticed a single word embroidered on the image: R.O.N.I.N.

"Ronin?" he loudly blurted. "What's ronin?"

Hearing his brother, Mitch snapped out of his data trance. "Ronin? Isn't that the name given to Japanese samurai who no longer serve a master? Mostly they're soldiers of fortune, I think. Or bandits. . . ."

"In this particular case, that definition of this 'R.O.N.I.N.' is not correct," a familiar voice declared.

Tom and Mitch turned and hardly blinked at the ornate brass cage descending from a shaft in the ceiling. After what they'd seen already, a secret elevator didn't have much of an impact.

"If you knew there was an elevator, why did you make us use those crummy stairs?" Mitch griped. The cage bumped to a halt and Mr. Chance stepped out. His reply was an amused smile.

"Forget the elevator!" Tom cried. "You said something about R.O.N.I.N."

Mr. Chance shook his head. "R-O-N-I-N is a highly secret organization that is tied in with your family's history. This place is your father's *real* office."

"What?" Tom stared blankly.

"Mr. Chance, Dad's a businessman," Mitch said levelly. "He sells digital equipment internationally."

"That is correct. That is also his *cover*," Mr. Chance replied.

"Cover?" Mitch repeated. "What do you mean—"

"Like *secret* cover?" Tom interrupted in confusion. "Like a spy or something? Like a CIA guy?"

"You're not saying Dad's a secret agent for the

government?" Mitch asked. "Are you?"

"Not precisely," Mr. Chance said. "You see, our modern acronym, R.O.N.I.N., stands for Rogue Operative Network Inter-National. We are not part of any nation or government. The Rogue Operative Network Inter-National battles evil and injustice wherever it is found around the world, for the betterment of all nations."

"I've never heard of that," Mitch said. "Secret agents without a country?"

"R.O.N.I.N. was created hundreds of years ago," Mr. Chance explained. "But the principles of truth, honor, and justice that guide R.O.N.I.N. are far more ancient."

Tom sighed. "Sorry . . . I just . . . I don't get it. You're saying our dad, and you . . . and this place . . . it's all a part of some worldwide organization?"

Mr. Chance smiled patiently. "The story of R.O.N.I.N. began nearly four centuries ago in the days of the samurai. A great and noble lord was murdered by a corrupt government official. The samurai who served the murdered lord had no master and became ronin."

"Hey!" Mitch protested. "You said my definition was wrong, but that's the same story I remember!"

Mr. Chance stared at the ceiling. "If you continue to interrupt me, this could take quite a long time to explain."

Tom signaled his motormouthed brother to zip it.

"The forty-seven samurai warriors who served the murdered man secretly vowed to bring the corrupt official to justice," Mr. Chance continued, "though it meant certain death to all of them."

"Wait a minute! I know this story," Tom cried.

"You should," Mr. Chance replied. "I told their story to you when you were children."

"Well, could you remind me how it ends?" Tom asked.

"Come on, you remember," Mitch insisted. "To fool the corrupt official, the forty-seven samurai renounced their warrior heritage and took up normal lives as tradesmen, farmers, and fishermen. Some even pretended to be drunks and bandits. But what they were really doing was spying on the official, waiting for the perfect time to mete out justice for murdering their lord."

"Yeah, I remember now," said Tom. "They got the bad guy in the end, but it was a suicide mission."

"It's called *seppuku*," Mitch put in.

"Back then I preferred the happier bedtime stories Mr. Chance used to tell us—the ones about Captain Kirk and Mr. Spock," Tom said.

"That's probably because you were too young to know he was feeding us episodes of an old television show." Mitch stared at his brother. "You do *know* that, don't you, Tom?"

Mr. Chance cleared his throat. "What you remember about the ronin story is true. But what you do not know is that each of those forty-seven samurai left a scroll behind—a scroll filled with the knowledge and wisdom each of them attained during their lifetime as warriors dedicated to justice."

He placed one hand on each of their shoulders. "I want to show you something."

Mr. Chance steered them to a wall dominated by a large portrait of their grandfather in his Marine Corps uniform. Tom and Mitch hardly remembered the general. He lived through some harrowing battles in the Pacific during World War II but died around the same time as their mother, when the boys were still very young.

Mr. Chance reached out and touched the picture frame. The portrait slid to one side, revealing a secret compartment. Behind bulletproof glass was an ancient scroll, brown with age. The yellowing parchment was covered with delicately rendered kana characters.

"This is the scroll given into your grandfather's care when he was initiated into R.O.N.I.N. in Japan, after World War II. Shortly thereafter your grandfather returned to America, and with this scroll he resurrected an ancient clan of R.O.N.I.N."

Mr. Chance gestured to the gold shield across the room. The three-bladed dagger gleamed at its center.

"Clan?" Mitch repeated.

"There are always forty-seven clans. No more. No less. They are located all over the world, in all cultures, among all races. If any one clan should fall, a new one rises to take its place. The initiation ceremony is an ancient one, full of ritual."

Mr. Chance gestured to the banner displaying the jade dragon. "Only the leader of R.O.N.I.N. knows the names of all of the members and where they are located."

"Who's the leader of R.O.N.I.N.?" asked Mitch.

"He is called the Dragon. Only an elite few know who he is, and what name he was born with."

Mr. Chance gestured again to the banner in the center of the room, which displayed the jade dragon. "And the most sacred scroll is known as the Dragon Scroll. It carries the secret knowledge of the clan locations and identities. It is the most important scroll of all."

"And you're saying our dad's a member of one of this . . . this rogue network's clans?" Tom asked.

"He is the *leader* of a clan, young sirs, just as your grandfather was. Just as, one day, you both are meant to be."

"Us!" Mitch cried. "Wait a second!"

"Yeah, back up," Tom agreed. He was usually the guy to plow right ahead without questions, but not now—this was just too freaking much!

"It is your father's destiny to serve the cause of justice," Mr. Chance told them, "as it is yours, should you accept it."

Mitch blew out air and began to pace. "Is this why Dad's missing? Is he in trouble? In some kind of danger . . . because of this . . . this R.O.N.I.N. stuff?"

Mr. Chance's unreadable mask never cracked. "I have not heard from your father since you last spoke with him," he said softly. "But please do not fret, young sirs. Things like this have happened before, and your father is a most resourceful agent. I am sure he will be home soon, safe and sound."

The brothers absorbed the news in silence, but their minds were racing as dozens of inexplicable events from their past suddenly made sense.

Tom recalled the time their father returned from a

business trip with a broken arm and bruises on his face. He blamed it on a clumsy fall down a flight of stairs. Tom now realized that their father had probably been on a mission—a rough one.

Mitch recalled a trip to the American Museum of Natural History many years before. Early on, he'd noticed a strange man following them. Later, while he and Tom gazed in awe at the dinosaur skeletons, their father disappeared. Mr. Chance, who hadn't gone to the exhibit with them, suddenly appeared to escort them home.

"Your father was called away on business," Mr. Chance had explained at the time. But that night Mitch couldn't sleep. He heard the front door open and snuck downstairs. His father was there, clothes torn, wearing a grim, almost frightening expression that Mitch hadn't seen before or since.

"Don't worry," Mitch heard his father tell Mr. Chance. "No one will threaten my family again. . . ."

With that memory came a new question.

"What about our mother?" he asked. "Was *she* a rogue operative too?"

Mr. Chance frowned, then glanced at his watch. His eyes bulged in mock surprise. "Goodness, look at the hour! There is more to tell you . . . but *another* time. Go to bed now, I have work to do."

"You've got to be kidding!" Tom cried.

Mr. Chance shook his head. "I must implement additional security procedures to ward off more intruders. It's best you both go to your rooms, even if you don't go to sleep. And I caution you not to mention any of this to your friends or *anyone*—you will only put their lives, and yours, in danger."

"Wait a second!" exclaimed Mitch. "You can't drop something this massive on our heads and then just leave us hanging. What about these Black Lotus ninjas? Why are they after us? Are they enemies of R.O.N.I.N. or something? And what about this whole 'clan' thing . . . what clan is Dad's, who else is a member of it? And what is all this equipment for, anyhow? And what mission is he on and where?"

Mr. Chance's unperturbed gaze shifted from Mitch to Tom. Once again his stoic expression gave nothing away.

"Right," Tom said, folding his arms. "What Mitch said . . . and I have questions too—"

With a raised hand, Mr. Chance silenced them both. "Questions are the seeds of knowledge. But in any field, answers emerge in due time, after due diligence."

Mitch and Tom exchanged dubious glances. "Huh?"

"If you like, I can give you a ride back up on the elevator," Mr. Chance said as he entered the cage. "It's an antique, but I keep it in tip-top shape."

Tom shook his head.

"No thanks," Mitch snapped in frustration. "We'll stick with the stairs."

The boys climbed the stairs in silence, still trying to wrap their heads around what they had just learned.

CHAPTER 7

"This is way bizarre," Tom said as they moved back through the dank old tunnel.

Like a computer suddenly crammed with too much data, the brothers were still trying to process everything they'd learned.

"This is more than way bizarre," Mitch replied. "On a scale of one to ten it's a twelve."

"More like a twenty," said Tom. "But you have to admit, it's also sort of . . . cool."

"Cool?" Mitch muttered. "What's cool about it? Dad's been lying to us for fifteen years. Well, maybe not fifteen, but at least ten."

"Yeah, but we can forgive that, can't we?" Tom asked.

"And Mr. Chance is enjoying being as inscrutable as Confucius," Mitch griped.

"I'm sure he has his reasons," countered Tom.

"And this whole R.O.N.I.N. thing throws a real monkey wrench into my ten-year plan!"

Tom rolled his eyes. "Not the ten-year plan again."

Mitch ticked off the highlights: "Advanced degrees in computer science and physics; video game designing and robotics on the side; contracts with Microsoft and LucasArts before I'm twenty-five."

"That's you," said Tom. "What about me?"

"What about you? You don't like planning your next meal, let alone your next decade."

"That's not true. After high school, I figured I'd spend a few seasons on the pro snowboarder circuit, then I was going to . . . you know . . . study video game design too."

"Just like me? How original."

"It's a good plan," Tom said. "We could have done it together."

"What do you mean, 'could have'?" asked Mitch.

"It's called the past tense, genius," Tom said. "Now that we know about Dad . . . and Granddad . . . I think we owe it to them to at least consider the family business, don't you?"

"You mean R.O.N.I.N.?" Mitch replied.

"Well, I don't mean digital equipment sales."

Mitch sighed, but he didn't argue. It was pointless anyway. They'd just reached the top of the old staircase.

The secret door opened automatically, and they stepped back into Mitch's basement workshop.

As the door slid closed behind them, Tom rubbed his chin. "I wonder how this thing works."

"Probably a hidden motion detector," guessed Mitch.

"How do we open it again?" Tom wondered, waving his hand in front of it. Nothing happened.

"We have other problems, you know," Mitch reminded his brother, pointing to the mess left behind after the confrontation.

Tom's mood darkened when he saw the remains of his laptop. "So much for my homework assignment." He groaned. "Guess I'll have to rewrite my paper, unless you can rescue the data on that hard drive."

Mitch glanced at the debris scattered on the floor. "Sorry, dude. Not even Bill Gates and a team of crack technicians could put this back together again."

Tom grunted. More bad news. Then he noticed another pile of debris in the corner of the garage.

"Sorry to tell you, bro, but it looks like you lost something too."

Mitch waved the loss away. "It's a piece of junk. Just a sonar system I designed to measure tides."

"That sounds high tech," said Tom.

"Not high tech enough," Mitch said with a sigh. "It was my entry in last year's Citywide Science Fair. But I lost to that girl, Laura Ting, as you already know."

Tom shook his head, still bugged about his laptop. "If she's so smart, maybe *she* can retrieve my homework out of this mess."

"If Bill Gates can't, no one can. Actually, now that you mention it, though, her family does own a computer store, Ting Microsystems—"

Mitch froze. Then his lips moved, but no sound came out.

"You're out of it, man. I'll admit the day's been rough, but we both have to snap out of it!"

Mitch's blue eyes met his brother's. "Did you hear what I said?"

Tom nodded. "That Laura Ting's family owns a computer store? Okay, so what's the big—"

"Ting Microsystems—*TM*!"

Mitch reached into his pocket and found the blue plastic thumb-drive cap. Tom saw it and understood immediately.

"You think she's connected?" asked Tom.

Mitch nodded. "The hair makes sense to me now!"

"What hair? What are you talking about?" Tom demanded.

"During the subway fight, the stranger didn't just drop this cap. He pulled a long black ponytail loose from his jacket. I thought it was really long for a dude, but I didn't put it all together until now."

Tom blinked. "I'm glad it makes sense to you. Now explain it to me."

"That skinny kid with the mask, Tom! The kid in the subway—"

"The dude who helped us fight the ninja?"

"I don't think he was a dude at all. I'm betting that masked stranger was Laura Ting, the girl who won first prize at last year's science fair!"

A minute later Mitch burst through the bedroom door and scrambled to his trophy shelf. He found last year's Citywide Science Fair program book tucked behind the already faded second-prize ribbon he'd won. Falling across his bed, he thumbed through the pages. Tom slumped down on the bed, his face a mask of frustrated confusion.

"Look, it's all right here!" Mitch cried, displaying the program. "Laura Ting's family owns a computer business in Manhattan. And see her picture. She has a long, black ponytail!"

Tom nodded. "Maybe. But you could be wrong. There could be other explanations for the TM and the ponytail. And do you really think a teenage girl could beat a Black Lotus ninja—whatever that is?"

Mitch sat up. "I think I'm right, Tom. We have to at least talk to Laura Ting. If it was her, then it's like she was following us, like she knew the ninja was going to attack. And if she knew *that*, she probably knows a whole lot more, right?"

"That's a stretch. Maybe she was just spying on your progress."

"Huh?"

"Maybe she wanted to glom onto the secret of your Citywide Science Fair project, so she could whup your butt again."

Mitch snorted. "I'm serious, man. This is not a joke."

Tom shrugged. "Okay. Even if it was her, maybe she was just riding the subway, saw us in trouble, and thought she'd help out. You know, kind of a good Samaritan thing."

"You'd have to be a *great* Samaritan—or absolutely nuts—to square off against a ninja," replied Mitch. "That's why I think Laura Ting had a reason to help us. I have a feeling she's somehow involved in whatever's happening, and she knows something we don't."

Tom shook his head. "What do you think, *she's* a rogue operative too?"

"I don't know, I don't know," muttered Mitch, eyes distant.

WHO NEEDS JET LI?
THIS DUDE ROCKS!

SAVED BY A HISTORY
ASSIGNMENT!

MR. CHANCE CAN'T BE GONE . . .
HE HAD TO HAVE KNOWN.

"For lack of a better theory, I'll humor you," Tom said. "Laura Ting's involved. So what do we do next?"

"First we find the address of her family's business. Then we pay Laura Ting a visit," Mitch replied, while he paged through the phone book.

"Here's the listing!" he cried. "Ting Microsystems on Mott Street."

"Whoa. Mott Street is w-a-a-a-y downtown," Tom warned. "We're going to have to take the subway."

"Right," said Mitch. "So I guess we'll go in the morning, right after breakfast."

"You know what?" Tom stood up. "I don't eat breakfast. I say we go *now*."

"Wait a second!" Mitch cried, suddenly nervous. "It's eleven o'clock. Practically the middle of the night. We can't go out now."

"Then we'll *never* get out," Tom declared. "Do you really think Mr. Chance is going to let us out of his sight after what happened today? No way. We're homebound until school on Monday morning. Maybe longer. Maybe forever."

Mitch's shoulders sagged. "Yeah, I didn't think of that."

Tom's eyes gleamed. "But if we go tonight, I think we can get past him. You heard Mr. Chance. He's going to be 'implementing new security procedures,' right?

That means he'll be busy the whole night. While he's distracted, we can sneak out of the house."

Mitch rubbed the back of his neck. "I don't know . . . I have to think about this."

"Climb down off that fence, genius!" exclaimed Tom. "It's time to act, not think. I don't know about you, but I'm sick of having one ninja after another in my face. And you want to find out what's going on, don't you?"

"Sure I do."

"Then it's now or never."

Mitch stood. "All right, you win. But let's put on dark clothing so we can blend into the scenery."

"Good idea," agreed Tom. "And don't forget your Pocket Pal. I have a feeling you're going to need it."

CHAPTER 8

Escaping the house was a no-brainer. Mr. Chance had yet to activate the burglar alarm, so Tom and Mitch simply slipped right out through the front door—*Buh-bye!*

"Do you think he'll notice we're gone?" Tom asked as they jogged through the nighttime streets.

Mitch shook his head. "I stuffed two ski suits with socks and shirts and used soccer balls for heads. Mr. Chance will have to pull down the blankets to figure out that's not us in our beds."

Tom grinned. "With all your science fair inventions and advanced technology, that's the best cover you could come up with, brainiac?"

"Hey!" Mitch defended himself. "I didn't exactly have a lot of time to prepare. Besides, sometimes the oldest tricks work the best."

"I hope you're right, bro," said Tom.

The night was cold and damp, but the fresh air smelled great after that dank underground tunnel. *Still* . . . Mitch couldn't shake the feeling that they were being followed.

"Let's head over to Grand Central," he suggested, glancing back over his shoulder. "From there we can catch the six train to Chinatown."

After the crazy day they'd had so far, Mitch thought he'd be more nervous, especially since they'd disobeyed Mr. Chance *big-time.* Yet the hint of danger gave him a real rush of excitement.

Neither Mitch nor his brother had ever roamed the midnight streets alone like this. He was amazed at how night transformed the entire city. Nothing seemed familiar. Streets they walked along every day were now aglow with lights and signs and doorways they'd never noticed before.

As they neared midtown, Tom hooked into the energy of the crowd. People leaving shows, going to restaurants or clubs, were so full of excitement they seemed to radiate a contagious electricity.

Mitch was pumped too, with the kind of buzz he felt when he accomplished a really difficult science project— or pulled off some truly awesome prank, usually on his brother.

Maybe being a rogue agent isn't such a bad thing after all, Mitch decided. Danger, excitement, the thrill of the unknown . . . it's kind of like experimental physics.

But when the brothers descended into the subway, different emotions took hold. The platform was much emptier than it had been during rush hour. There were a few hollow-eyed vagrants sleeping on benches or lurking in the shadows. Echoing sounds boomed hollowly through pitch-black tunnels, as if strange creatures were creeping around, just beyond the light's reach.

Tom and Mitch nervously looked over their shoulders. By the time they boarded the number six train, they both felt jumpy and paranoid.

Perched on the edge of his seat in the nearly empty subway car, Mitch realized that Mr. Chance had been right about one thing: He and his brother really *were* starting to view the world differently.

At the Canal Street station, the boys got off the train. The temperature had dropped, and the sky looked heavy with clouds. As Tom and Mitch emerged from the subway stairs, it began to drizzle. They buttoned their dark-colored jackets and pulled their sweatshirt hoods over their heads.

They were now in the heart of New York City's Chinatown district, a very old section of the city. Its narrow cobblestone streets were lined with markets, tiny shops, and cramped restaurants. There were multicolored paper lanterns dangling in front of many stores. Signs were written in Chinese characters. As they turned onto Mott Street, even the architecture and the ornate building facades evoked the feeling of a continent half a world away.

At such a late hour, most businesses on this quiet stretch were closed. The light drizzle turned into a steady rain, and the air was no longer refreshingly bracing—it was just plain *cold*. Crossing deserted Mott Street, Mitch and Tom shivered under their jackets.

Mitch halted, glanced at the yellow page torn from the phone book. "This is the right address," he said.

Tom blinked in surprise. Under a faded Ting Microsystems sign, graffiti-etched steel shutters covered the windows and door. On the second floor, the windows were covered too—boarded up with plywood as if a hurricane were coming. The windows on the third floor weren't covered, but they were pitch-black.

Tom didn't try to hide his disappointment. "Ting Microsystems sure doesn't live up to its impressive name. In fact, I think they might have gone bankrupt."

"It looks deserted, but let's make sure." Mitch led his brother down a narrow, debris-strewn alley to the back of the building. It was so dark he used the flashlight on his Pocket Pal to navigate around Dumpsters filled to the brim with reeking garbage. They heard scurrying noises and the squeal of rats.

"I don't know which I like better—the smell, the vermin, or the weather," Tom complained, holding his nose.

"Look," said Mitch. "The back door has a steel gate, but none of the upstairs windows are boarded up."

"There's the fire escape, too." Tom grinned. "This is going to be easy. Let's go."

Mitch remained rooted to the spot. "Go where?"

"Inside, dude. Don't be so dense. We can use the fire escape to get to the upstairs, then climb through the window—"

"That's a crime, Tom. Haven't you ever heard of breaking and entering?"

Tom shrugged. "I'll be real careful. Anyway, I think it's only entering, if I don't actually *break* anything."

"I think you're the dense one now."

Just then, Mitch thought he saw a light behind an upstairs window. It appeared and then vanished in a wink.

"Wait! I think someone is in there," he whispered.

"It's deserted. You said so yourself," Tom declared as he yanked down the fire escape ladder. "Don't wimp out on me now, brainiac."

CHAPTER 9

The fire escape was old and creaky, its railings pitted with rust and flaking paint. With each step the brothers took, the entire contraption wobbled and groaned. When they reached the second floor, Tom squinted through the window, using his flashlight to pierce the darkness.

"This isn't very safe," whispered Mitch in a shaky voice.

"Relax," Tom whispered back. "We're no higher than the tallest diving board at Astoria Pool, and you're not afraid to jump off *that.*"

"Yeah, the pool is filled with water. That's a *concrete* alley down there."

Tom shrugged. "If you slip, just aim for that Dumpster. It's filled with plastic garbage bags. They'll break your fall."

"Gross." Mitch shuddered. "I can smell it from here—and I'd rather take my chances with the concrete."

"This window isn't locked," Tom said, testing the frame.

Mitch peeked over his brother's shoulder. "What do you see in there?" he asked.

"A lot of boxes and stuff. Ting Microsystems might be deserted, but the place isn't empty." Tom tried to raise the window and failed. He examined the frame, then frowned. "It's stuck. But if I chip some of the old paint away, I think I can jimmy it open."

"If there's a burglar alarm, you might set it off," Mitch cautioned.

"If we hear a siren, we'll run away as fast as we can."

"What if it's a silent alarm?"

Tom rolled his eyes. "Then we'll run away silently, nerd-o. Now hold the light steady and let me get to work."

While Mitch held his own flashlight, Tom unfolded the tools hidden inside his Pocket Pal. Using the screwdriver, he began chipping away at the ancient paint. Mitch fidgeted nervously, sure every siren he heard in the distance was gaining on them.

"Got it," Tom declared at last. The window rattled as it opened—so loudly it sounded like an explosion in the quiet night. Tom crawled right through. Mitch followed, relieved to be off the rickety fire escape.

They found themselves on a narrow cast-iron catwalk suspended over the main shopping floor of the computer store. The ornate walkway probably dated from the nineteenth century, but Mitch figured it would be a pretty handy place to watch for shoplifters.

Boxes of merchandise were stacked on tall aluminum racks around them. Down below, display shelves held merchandise—cell phones, alarm clocks, digital cameras, battery chargers, MP3 players, desktop computers, and laptops.

Tom found the ladder. "I'm going down," he whispered.

He had just placed his foot on the first rung, when Mitch heard a sound from above. He looked up and spied a black shape crouched on a stack of boxes.

"Watch out, Tom!" Mitch warned—too late.

The shadowy figure leaped from the perch and slammed into his brother. Mitch watched in horror as Tom and the attacker both tumbled off the ladder to the floor below.

Tom had heard Mitch's cry a split second before the figure struck him. He saw stars, then felt the rung slip out from under his feet. Determined not to take the plunge alone, he held on to the squirming figure.

"Let me go!" The voice was high-pitched and furious.

They landed with a crash on top of the counter. Tom gasped as the wind was knocked out of him. Thankfully, they had landed on wood, not glass. Instead of shattering, the counter merely caved in under their weight. The cash register tumbled to the floor with a loud bang.

Battered, Tom managed to stand. He whirled to find his attacker crouched and spoiling for a fight. The figure was clad in black, face masked by a dark hood. Tom aimed for the chin and lashed out with a high kick.

As slippery as liquid mercury, the figure ducked under the blow and delivered a spinning kick that swept Tom's legs out from under him. He crashed to the floor.

Tom heard Mitch's voice from the catwalk. "Wait! Stop! There's no reason to fight," his brother cried.

No way am I going to surrender! Tom thought. As long as this guy's in my face, I'm going to fight.

The figure loomed over him, fist raised. In one smooth motion, Tom rolled aside and kick-jumped to his feet. The fist descended and struck the floorboards, and they split with a loud *snap*. Tom heard a girly-sounding yelp of surprise. Though his fists were raised and he was ready to rumble, this time he didn't press the attack.

Meanwhile, Mitch had scrambled down the ladder and threw himself between the fighters.

"Stop, stop! We're on the same side," he yelled.

The robed figure stepped back, out of reach. Then Laura Ting pulled the hood off her head. Her long hair spilled out like a blue-black waterfall. Eyes wary, legs braced, she stared at the intruders.

"What do you want?" she demanded, massaging sore knuckles.

"It's me. Mitch Hearn. This is my brother, Tom. You helped us on the subway platform today—I mean yesterday. Remember?"

She nodded.

Tom lowered his arms. "If you know who we are, why did you attack me?"

Mitch slapped his own forehead. "Think about it for a second. We broke into her family's shop. Of course Laura attacked us! She was just trying to protect herself."

"Oh, all of a sudden it's Laura this and Laura that. Whose side are you on?" Tom grumbled.

"I'm not on anybody's side—"

Tom wagged an accusing finger at Laura Ting. "She attacked *me*, in case you were daydreaming! I didn't want to hurt her. I didn't know who she was. She's lucky all that got bruised were her knuckles."

"Tough guy," Mitch shot back. "Beat up on a little girl."

"That 'little girl' knows kung fu—"

Laura Ting stamped her foot. "Shut up, both of you. You sound like my stupid brothers."

"Did your brothers teach you kung fu?" demanded Tom, still irritated that a girl almost beat him.

"It's Jeet Kune Do—not that either of you are skilled enough to recognize the difference," she replied.

The brothers exchanged guilty glances. Laura's remark was snarky, but she wasn't wrong. Both Mitch and Tom had taken plenty of martial arts lessons, but neither of them had worked hard enough to master the techniques.

"I attacked you because I thought you were more punks working for Julian Vane," Laura told them.

Mitch and Tom stared blankly. "Julian Vane? Who's Julian Vane?" Tom asked.

CHAPTER 10

At that very moment, on Manhattan's Upper West Side, the New York Philharmonic played its final flourish. The glamorous crowd exited the majestic Lincoln Center concert hall and swarmed toward the line of taxis and chauffeured limousines parked along Broadway.

In the middle of the mass exodus, ringed by tuxedoed bodyguards, one man stood out from the rest. Six feet tall from the tips of his Bruno Magli shoes to the top of his shaven head, the brawny gentleman had the appearance of an impeccably dressed Mr. Universe.

All smiles, he shook the proffered hands of the rich and famous, returning their courteous greetings. A well-known supermodel and cover girl, dazzling in a haute couture gown, clung to his muscular arm, cheerfully nodding.

A bold paparazzo slipped through the mob and snapped the couple's photograph. Mr. Universe continued walking and smiling but made a simple gesture, whereupon his bodyguards pulled the photographer into the shadows.

Two bullyboys held him, while a third smashed his digital camera against the concrete plaza.

"Hey, that camera cost a lot of money," the photographer complained. One bodyguard whirled to face the photographer, who stepped back fearfully. The thug reached into the pocket of his tuxedo and tossed a fistful of hundred-dollar bills at the man's feet.

"Next time leave Mr. Vane alone," the hired thug warned.

A moment later the entourage reached a black Rolls-Royce. A uniformed driver opened the door. The supermodel moved to climb inside, when she was suddenly shoved backward by her own date.

"She needs a taxi," Julian Vane ordered his driver.

"But Mr. Vane," the model exclaimed, "Julian! I thought we were hitting it off!"

"No, my dear," said Vane. "Notwithstanding your ability to hold up a fashionable dress, I find you a tedious, vapid bore."

The door closed in her face and the car sped away. In the spacious back of the limo, Vane stretched his long legs. As he poured himself a drink, his cell phone buzzed once, and he placed it to his ear.

"Speak."

"It's Roman Maldeen, Mr. Vane," an uneasy voice replied.

"Do you have the boys?"

A pause followed. "The ninja infiltrated the house through the underwater tunnel, but he was attacked by Mr. Chance and couldn't complete the mission."

Vane's thin lips curled into an angry sneer. "Chance. I should have known he'd be loyal till the end. I am very disappointed, Mr. Maldeen. Your ninjas have failed me twice. If you can't get the job done this time, there won't be any other chances. Do you understand?"

"Yes, sir."

Vane brushed lint from his lapel. "And the other matter?"

"The Ting family have fled their shop on Mott Street," Roman Maldeen replied. "But I'm confident I can locate the processor within the next twenty-four hours."

"If you know what's best for you, you will not disappoint me again, Mr. Maldeen."

侍

Laura Ting poured dark, aromatic tea into three small porcelain cups. In the dull glow of the crank-powered emergency lantern, Mitch watched the steam rise in a cloud around her delicate features.

She handed a cup to Tom, then gave one to Mitch. Her soft hands brushed his fingers as he accepted the cup.

They sat in a circle on the rug, in a tiny break area for Ting Microsystems employees on the third floor. A frayed blanket lay across the sagging couch where Laura had been sleeping when they broke in.

The wind blew, and rain spattered the grimy window. The girl set the pot down next to the battery-operated hot plate and shivered slightly under her thick sweater.

"My father is a genius," Laura began. "Not that he has fancy degrees or anything. But he understands things, you know? Especially computer technology."

She spoke softly, almost in a whisper. "That's why my father opened this computer sales and repair shop. My brothers aren't interested in science or technology, not like I am. All they care about are fast cars and working out at the dojo. My father and I, we share something special. But when I was about seven years old, my father hired this guy, Julian Vane, to manage the store. For years they were great friends, and Julian was treated like a part of the family. Then he became more and more greedy; all he wanted was power and money. Then one day he made a deal with my dad: He was going to market this invention of my father's using some connections he had made over the years. He said he could make my dad famous, and make the business tons of money. My father agreed, and then Vane ran off with the invention, marketed it as his own, and made millions of dollars. We never saw a penny of it. I haven't heard anything about him in years, but I always had my suspicions that he'd be back for more."

Laura turned the cup in her hand. "Three weeks ago, my dad told me he'd invented something, right here in his workshop, that would change computers forever: the fastest, smallest processor ever made. It is just a tiny chip, but it can perform the work of a giant mainframe computer."

"Phew!" whistled Mitch.

"Dad said he was ready to market the invention, but he had to go out of town first, visit with one of our store's big clients for a few days." Laura shook her head. "It didn't make any sense to me. As far as I knew, we didn't have any out-of-town clients! But Dad went to the airport the next day, and that's the last time anyone in our family has seen him."

Tom and Mitch exchanged glances. Their own father had left on business around that same time—then vanished, too. It seemed too neat to be a coincidence.

"Before he left, my dad told me he'd hidden the prototype processor and the plans to manufacture it somewhere in this shop," Laura continued. "He said they were hidden in a place close to his heart, and that if anything should happen to him, I was to find the device and market it to a big corporation to support the family."

Laura wiped a tear away quickly, so they wouldn't notice. The boys pretended they didn't.

"A couple of days ago, some guy named Roman Maldeen and a bunch of goons pulled up in front of our shop in a limousine so big it could hardly drive down Mott Street. I could see why he needed such a big car. Maldeen was, like, seven feet tall—the guy was a giant. He said he worked for Julian Vane. Surprise, surprise."

Laura paused. "The whole scene was pretty scary. I was alone with Mom, who was working at the register. Maldeen came in, roaring in a loud voice that Dad had sold his boss the patent for the new high-tech chip. He demanded that we turn the processor and the schematics over to him at once."

Laura gulped her tea. Her eyes were bright.

"My mom was in shock. She knew nothing about the invention; my dad only told me about it, and no one else. I was furious; there was no way I was going to let history repeat itself. I'm my father's only hope."

"What did you do?" Tom asked.

"I played dumb, even when his three bodyguards pushed my mom around and busted up the shop. What else could I do? It's not like I could tell him where the chip was—I didn't know then, and I don't know now."

Laura's spine stiffened, and her voice became hard. "Vane had something to do with my father's disappearance, otherwise he wouldn't know about the processor. Julian Vane must know where my dad is."

Mitch set his empty cup on the floor. "So, how powerful is Julian Vane?"

"Very," Laura replied. "He's a business tycoon. Half the articles praise his 'genius' and the other half condemn him as a corporate raider without a conscience."

She chewed her finger. "What did that one article say? Oh, yeah! The prime minister of the Republic of Malagana claims Julian Vane wrecked his country's economy by messing with the value of its currency. He walked away with close to a billion dollars, but he ruined Malagana's businesses and put more than half its people out of work. Minister Mbuto called him 'an economic vampire who feeds on human suffering.'"

"Sounds like a really nice guy," said Tom.

"A lot of people actually think he is," Laura replied. "Vane is also an internationally famous philanthropist. He's always throwing parties for politicians and celebrities. He hosted a charity event at Lincoln Center this very evening."

"So what did this 'philanthropist' do next?" Mitch asked.

"After his punks left, I wanted to call the police. But my mom is old school, she's afraid to get the authorities involved. Anyway, my brothers were closing up the store that night when the ninjas showed up—"

"Ninjas!" Tom cried. "You mean like—"

Laura nodded. "Like the guy who attacked you. Only a whole bunch of them. They tied my brothers up and searched the store. My oldest brother, Jesse, slipped out of his bonds and freed Benny. The ninjas were still searching the store when they escaped. They brought back the cops, but the sirens spooked them, and they took off."

Laura hugged her sweater tightly. "After that, my family moved across the river, to stay with relatives in New Jersey. My brothers had the store boarded up and the power cut off, hoping Vane and his gangsters would leave us alone."

Tom appeared skeptical. "If your family moved to Jersey, how come you're here now?"

Even in the dim light, Tom and Mitch could see Laura's pale face flushing red. "I ran away three days ago," she confessed. "That's why I ran off after the police came for the ninja. I didn't want them to find out I was a runaway. They would just make me go back home—but I have to finish what I started. My father's invention, his legacy, is somewhere in this shop. I've got to find it before Vane does!"

"So why were you following us in the first place?" Mitch asked.

"I knew where you went to school—it said so in the science fair program book. But it didn't say where you lived," Laura explained. "I followed you down to that computer store, then back uptown again. When that ninja attacked . . . Well, I had to do something, right?"

Mitch was confused. "I still don't get it. Why did you need to know where we lived?"

Laura seemed puzzled by the question. "My dad doesn't have many friends in New York. Actually, he doesn't have *any* friends. But since he knew your father—"

"What?" Tom cried.

"It's true. I'm certain our dads knew each other, because I saw them both talking at the science fair last year. They sat together for a long time."

Mitch searched his memory of the event, but he soon realized he'd been so busy making sure his sonar invention worked that he hadn't noticed anything else.

"I figured that since your dad knows mine, maybe your father knows where my father went when he disappeared," Laura told them.

Mitch and Tom exchanged glances. "Tell her," Tom commanded.

So Mitch told Laura that their own father had

vanished, too, around the same time as her father disappeared.

"That's just too weird to be a coincidence," Laura concluded. "There must be a connection."

They sat in silence for a moment.

"Are you sure your father's invention is really here?" Mitch asked.

Laura frowned. "I looked everywhere for the prototype. Dad said he kept it close to his heart, and he had a lot of lab coats, jackets, and shirts hanging around. I searched lapel pockets—all the pockets, in fact—and found nothing. But I know he wouldn't lie to me. It has to be here somewhere!"

"Maybe the ninjas found it," suggested Tom.

Laura shook her head stubbornly. "It's *here*. I can feel it. I—"

They were interrupted by a loud twang, followed by a grunt of pain. Tom looked up in time to see a silhouette on the other side of the window. Almost immediately, the form dropped out of sight.

Tom ran to the window. He found an empty rope turning in the wind. Mitch and Laura peered over his shoulder. In the Dumpster in the alley far below, they spied a masked man dressed from head to toe in black. He sprawled, unmoving, across a pile of stinking garbage.

"The ninjas are back," Tom whispered.

"But what happened to him?" wondered Mitch. "Did he slip off the rope?"

"A klutzy ninja?" Tom said. "Right, *that* makes sense. . . . Hey, look!" He pointed to something laying on top of the garbage next to him.

"An arrow?" Mitch asked.

"That's a crossbow bolt," Tom corrected. "A regular arrow would be much longer."

"Okay," said Mitch, "so he was shot down with a crossbow. But who did the shooting?"

The brothers exchanged worried glances.

"That's it," Mitch stated, turning from the window. "We're going home, and Laura, you're coming with us."

Tom blinked in surprise and faced his brother. "Are you sure that's a good idea? I mean, she's not a pet turtle. You can't hide her in your room. How do we explain her to Mr. Chance?"

"I'll think of something," promised Mitch.

"Maybe I don't want to go," Laura said, folding her arms and glaring at the brothers.

Mitch put a hand on her shoulder. "You can't stay. Ninjas are lurking all around this place—"

"Which means they haven't found my father's invention."

"So we'll come back and look for it in the daytime," Mitch replied.

"You might want to take a look at this," Tom called from the window. He pointed toward the alley. Mitch and Laura looked into the Dumpster again. The crossbow bolt was there. The ninja wasn't.

"Grab your backpack, Laura," cried Mitch. "We're getting out of here."

CHAPTER 11

Tom glanced over his shoulder. First Avenue was creepy this early in the morning. There were no pedestrians in sight. One lone car swept down the night-shrouded street, tires swishing on the wet pavement.

"Mitch, what's the problem?" he whispered, lowering his hood. He imagined ninjas lurking in every shadow. "It's taking you forever to pop that door, and it's cold out here."

Mitch was kneeling on the front step, trying to short-circuit the alarm system of their own townhouse. Carefully he probed the crack between the door and the doorjamb with the flex-wire attachment of his Pocket Pal.

"I don't want to hurry," Mitch said, wiping his brow. "I might actually trip the alarm instead of disabling it. And then we'll be busted."

Tom nodded. "You're right. Let's not get the Chance Man involved if we don't have to. I for one don't want to get grounded for eternity."

Laura Ting was slumped on the steps, weighed down by her heavy backpack. She looked exhausted from their difficult escape and the trip uptown.

Mitch figured they hadn't been followed, thanks to Laura's quick thinking. Instead of leaving Ting Microsystems by the fire escape, Laura showed them a secret exit in the basement of the building.

"It's an old coal cellar that leads to the sewers," she'd explained. "My brothers use it to sneak out of the shop and go drag racing in Queens."

"Cool! I think I'd like your brothers," Tom had said.

With Laura in the lead, they'd climbed through a metal hatch, then moved along a cobblestone coal chute that ran under the building. The tunnel—complete with squealing, scrabbling rats—ran to a sewage drain half a block away. High-powered electrical lines flowed like thick snakes along the walls on either side of them.

"Don't touch one. You might get fried," Laura had warned.

Eventually they'd squeezed through a storm drain on Mott Street, then sprinted all the way to the subway, which carried them within walking distance to their East Side home.

I just wish my genius brother could get us inside it! Tom thought.

"I'd like to know what happened to that ninja back at Laura's place," said Mitch, his eyes still fixed on the task of breaking and entering.

Tom shrugged. "I'm betting he was wearing some sort of meshed body armor. The fall is probably what knocked him out."

"Yeah . . . that makes sense," Mitch said. "I guess when he came to, he just took off."

"Right," Tom agreed.

Mitch scratched his head. "But it still doesn't explain *who* shot him."

Tom checked his watch. "I thought you said you'd bypassed this alarm system before."

"I did. Once," Mitch replied hotly. "But if you think you can do a better job, you're welcome to—"

The door abruptly opened. With a yelp, Mitch fell face-first across the threshold. Tom's jaw gaped in surprise. Laura Ting stifled a giggle.

Mr. Chance stood in the doorway, staring down at them.

"Ah, there you are," he said matter-of-factly. "Did you forget your key, young sirs?"

"I . . . er . . . that is, we—" Tom stammered.

"Come inside now, and change out of those damp clothes." Mr. Chance stepped aside to admit them. "Since you insisted on going out on this cold and rainy night, I've prepared a midnight snack for you and your guest."

Mitch quickly presented Laura to Mr. Chance. "This is Laura Ting. She's, uh . . . the first prize winner of last year's Citywide Science Fair."

It was just about the lamest introduction Mitch had ever made. But he couldn't think of what else to say. He figured he'd have till morning to come up with some kind of explanation.

"An honor to meet you, Ms. Ting." Mr. Chance bowed and shook Laura's hand. "Please escort the young lady to the guest room. It is ready to receive her. Refreshments await you in the dining area."

Tom caught Mitch's eye. "What's up?" he whispered. "Chance is acting like he expected us to walk in at two in the a.m.—and with Laura, too. Why isn't he asking where we were?"

The brothers stopped short at the base of the stairs. A medieval crossbow was leaning in plain sight against the wall.

Mr. Chance met their eyes and smiled.

"How careless of me to leave that lying around!" he said. "Please excuse me while I return it to the rack where it belongs."

Slinging the weapon over his shoulder, Mr. Chance headed for the basement.

Mitch gaped. "No wonder he didn't ask us where we were."

"Yeah," muttered Tom, his jaw slack too. "I guess now we know who shot the ninja."

侍

Tom passed Laura the serving bowl. "Try the tapioca pudding. It's awesome."

She wrinkled her nose. "You eat that stuff?"

Laura poured herself a cup of hot chocolate from the thermal carafe on the sideboard. Then she sat at the dining-room table, facing the brothers.

She'd changed into dry clothes she'd stuffed into her backpack—faded jeans and a T-shirt—and the transformation was so striking both boys found themselves staring.

Without the bulky urban gear, the fifteen-year-old was clearly a girl. Her straight, blue-black hair hung loose and was so long it swirled around her back. Her face was heart-shaped and pale, with large, expressive, almond-shaped eyes that carefully examined the details of her new surroundings.

"This is a really nice house," Laura said. "Makes me wonder how my dad knew yours. Different side of the subway tracks, you know what I mean?"

"Maybe they didn't know each other," Mitch suggested. "Maybe they were acquaintances that one day."

Laura shook her head. "My father bowed when he met your dad, which I thought was weird. I mean, my dad's polite and all, but he *never* bows."

She sighed and ran her delicate fingers through her long, silky hair like a supermodel doing a shampoo commercial. The brothers found themselves staring again. Laura caught them. "What are you looking at?"

"Nothing," they replied together.

Face flushed, Tom thrust his face back into his pudding bowl so fast he got tapioca on his nose. Mitch gulped hot chocolate—and burned his tongue.

Tom glanced at his brother, then spoke. "Laura, have you ever heard of R.O.N.I.N.?" he asked.

"Sure," she replied. "A ronin is some kind of samurai in those Japanese movies they show on the Independent Film Channel on Saturday mornings. But I don't watch that stuff. Too violent."

Tom shook his head. "Actually, I'm talking about a different kind of—"

His jaw shut when he saw Mitch's frantic chopping motion. Laura noticed the gesture and her eyes narrowed with suspicion.

"You were saying?" she asked pointedly.

Mitch jumped in quickly. "Tom was talking about

anime. He's a big fan of *Samurai Wind*."

Tom looked away. "Yeah, that's right," he said lamely. "I meant anime."

Laura frowned, looking hurt, but said nothing. They finished their snacks in silence, and Laura gave them a chilly good night.

"Smooth move," Mitch snapped when she was gone. "You almost told her about R.O.N.I.N. Now she thinks we're hiding something from her."

"We *are* hiding something from her, dude, and it isn't right," Tom shot back. "Laura's involved. I think she should know the truth."

"You think wrong, muscle-head," Mitch replied. "Remember what Mr. Chance said. We're not supposed to talk about R.O.N.I.N. Not to anyone."

"Yeah, right," Tom said with a dismissive wave.

"Look, I don't know much about being a secret agent," Mitch told him. "But one thing I know: The first rule of being a secret agent is that you never, ever tell anybody you're a secret agent, because—it's a *secret*!"

CHAPTER 12

The jade dragon marked the way, and Tom found himself stepping back inside the remote cave on the mysterious island.

In the flickering torchlight, he watched a man in a green robe walk once again into the cave's vast chamber from behind the hidden stone door. The hanging armor shifted, as if stirred by the ocean's winds gusting through the cave.

Wraithlike energies flowed upward from the glowing floor, until the ancient battle suit gleamed with an unnatural light. Soon the entire cavern radiated with an eerie emerald glow.

That's when he heard it—a far-off beating sound too modern to intrude on these surroundings. This rhythmic sound wasn't coming from any drum. The relentless beating came from the blades of helicopters!

From the cave's mouth, a voice boomed, "Protect the

Scroll!" For an insane instant, Tom thought the dragon had spoken. Then he felt a violent shaking. . . .

侍

"Tom! Wake up!"

He opened his eyes. Mitch was leaning over him, shaking his shoulders.

"She's gone," Mitch cried. "Laura Ting is gone!"

Tom sat up, instantly alert. "When?"

"I'm not sure. Probably last night. I knocked on her door first thing this morning. But she didn't answer, and when I opened the door she was gone!"

Tom threw off the sheets and rolled out of bed. "Mitch, are you sure she didn't just go down to breakfast or something?"

"Yes, I'm sure! She left us a note." Mitch held out a sheet of paper, torn from a school notebook.

Tom snatched the note and read. "She says she was wrong to leave her father's place without finding the processor. She says she's going back."

"Read the rest," urged Mitch.

"She says she knows we're hiding something from her, and if we can't be honest, she doesn't want our help. We should just leave her alone. . . . Oh, man."

Mitch clenched his fists. "What should we do?"

"We have to tell Mr. Chance," Tom replied.

"You already have," announced Mr. Chance. The

brothers whirled to find their butler standing in the doorway.

Tom confessed immediately. "I messed up bad, Mr. Chance. I mentioned something I shouldn't have, and now Laura doesn't trust us."

"We were trying to *help*. Couldn't she see that?" Mitch cried.

"Ms. Ting is wise for one so young. She does not give her trust so easily, even to you," Mr. Chance replied. "Laura Ting understands that deception goes hand in hand with conflict. But with deception comes distrust."

Mitch threw up his hands. "But we're trustworthy!"

Mr. Chance nodded. "You hid a greater truth, and that is a deception too."

Mitch frowned. "Then it *is* our fault she's gone."

"No," Mr. Chance declared. "You hid the truth in an effort to protect her, and shield yourselves. In war, everyone deceives. Allies even deceive one another—not to do harm, merely to achieve their own goals."

Mr. Chance's usual serene expression became suddenly intense. "Remember this," he warned. "In conflict, deception is everywhere. Nothing is what it seems."

Mitch got the feeling that Mr. Chance was trying to tell them something. But before he could question him, Tom spoke.

"So what do we do now? In her note Laura said she wants us to leave her alone."

Mr. Chance shook his head. "That we cannot do, for she is in very grave danger. We must proceed with caution, because this house is being watched–"

"Watched! By who?" Mitch asked. "Ninjas?"

Mr. Chance nodded somberly. "Never fear. I shall search for Ms. Ting in my car–"

"We're going too!" insisted Mitch.

Chance raised an eyebrow. "In your pajamas?" He turned to leave the room. "I suggest you dress first."

侍

Five minutes later Tom and Mitch were dressed in street clothes and on their way to the basement garage. They arrived in time to see Mr. Chance's silver PT Cruiser roll out of the townhouse.

"Wait!" Tom called, chasing the taillights up the ramp. Mitch was right behind him. Traffic was light, and the car swerved around the corner onto First Avenue without stopping.

By the time Tom reached the intersection, the Cruiser was half a block away. He faced Mitch.

"I can't believe the Chance Man left us be–"

They felt the blast before they heard it. The concussion washed over them, slamming Tom and Mitch down against the hard pavement. The bright autumn morning flashed white, like burning phosphorus. Finally the noise battered their ears, reverberating along the concrete corridor.

Mitch stumbled to his feet, then over to Tom. Smoke filled the wide avenue. Debris rained down. Car alarms howled. Someone screamed.

Mitch grabbed hold of his brother.

"It . . . it must have been a bomb," Tom said between coughs. His eyes were glassy with shock. "It just blew up. . . ."

Together they stumbled through the smoke and gathering crowd toward what was left of Mr. Chance's car, a tangle of burning wreckage sprawled across First Avenue. They felt the scorching heat as the flames blazed high. The smoke grew thicker and darker. In the distance, sirens wailed. Fire trucks, or the police—they couldn't tell.

"Do you see him?" Mitch called, choking and coughing from the smoke.

Tom held the hem of his sweatshirt over his mouth and nose. When he spoke, his voice was muffled. "No. There's nothing . . . no body. No skeleton. It's like he wasn't in the car. But where did he go?"

Mitch shook his head. "I don't know . . . maybe the blast blew him to bits. . . ."

"We have to find Mr. Chance!" cried Tom. He lunged

closer, until the fire licked at his clothing.

Mitch grabbed his brother and yanked him back. "No, Tom, use your head! You'll get hurt."

"But what about Mr. Chance—"

"He's gone. . . ."

CHAPTER 13

When Tom and Mitch returned to the garage, the secret door in the brick wall was open wide. The brothers took it as a sign from Mr. Chance that they shouldn't give up.

"He said we were being watched," Mitch said. "Mr. Chance should have planned for an attack. It isn't like him to be so careless."

Tom wiped tears from his cheeks. "Maybe he did plan for it. Maybe he wasn't in the car . . . or he got out somehow. Maybe we should just go to the police."

"And tell them what?" asked Mitch. "That ninjas are after us? That our dad's missing, but that's okay because he's part of some secret worldwide organization that they never heard of? They'll think we're loony tunes! They'll take us into custody, search our house, find all those weapons in the computer room, and accuse *us* of being kid terrorists who blew up the family car ourselves!"

Tom sighed and collapsed into a chair. "Fine, Mitch. What'll we do then? You're the brainiac. So think."

"Look, Tom, you didn't see Mr. Chance's body, so maybe he's gone, like I said—but *not* dead. We don't have any hard evidence for sure, so we have to hold it together. We need to find Dad. And the only one who has a connection to him now is Laura Ting. She thinks her dad might be with him."

"But Mr. Ting's missing too. So it's all speculation. Theories are fine, but someone's trying to kill us!" Tom jumped to his feet. "We've got to *act*!"

"Then let's find Laura," said Mitch. "We know she's in trouble, and we can step in and back her up. We can worry about everything else later."

Entering the secret door, they descended the stairs. Neither was surprised to find the door to the computer room open as well. The brothers chose their weapons carefully. Mitch selected the three-bladed dagger. He also picked a curved, double-edged throwing knife with a diamond-shaped weight in the center, linking the twin blades.

Mitch hefted the weapon and grinned. "This will do. It's lighter than the throwing star and perfectly balanced."

Tom chose a tonfa made of ornately carved teakwood. All black, the weapon resembled a police officer's nightstick with a handle projecting from the side—except that a curved blade had been added to the club. Two of these unique weapons hung on the rack. Tom took only one.

Next he selected a collapsible bow and a quiver of steel arrows. Mr. Chance had tutored both of the brothers at the archery range since they were very young. Twice a week they practiced. After years of training, Mitch was good with the bow, but Tom was phenomenal. He *never* missed the target, even with the heaviest bow. He was so good that when they studied archery in gym class, his teacher had Tom demonstrate the proper form for the rest of the students.

They used a gym bag, and a bow carrier, to stow their weapons. Under their jackets the brothers wore black ski sweatpants and T-shirts. The hiking boots they chose were left over from summer camp and were heavy enough to make every kick count.

Outside, they ignored the fire engines and police cars that had cordoned off the smoking wreck and hurried away.

侍

Chinatown's sidewalks were packed with Saturday shoppers too busy to do more than glance at a couple of teenage boys climbing into a storm drain.

Mitch dropped the gym bag down to Tom, then

joined him in the narrow drainage tunnel.

"Mind the wires," Mitch warned.

In the shafts of daylight streaming through grates and tiny openings in the manhole covers, the electrical lines appeared frayed and worn.

"It's the salt," explained Mitch. "In winter they use it to clear the snow and ice, but the salt flows down here with the water and rots the insulation."

"That's more information than I'll ever need on the subject, but thanks anyway, Mr. Science," Tom replied.

"Okay," said Mitch, "but if you fry yourself on a high-voltage wire, I get to say 'I told you so.'"

A few minutes later the brothers were climbing through the creaky metal coal hatch into the dank basement of Ting Microsystems. This time they tarried long enough to spot Mr. Ting's workshop in the corner. It was a tiny space crammed with gear and spools of copper wire—one of the best metal conductors, Mitch noted in passing.

As they approached the stairs, Mitch and Tom heard voices. Cautiously, they climbed the steps and peeked around the corner.

Though it was late morning outside, the shop's doors and windows were still shuttered by steel gates that blocked the sun. Ninjas wearing black, hooded battle suits and carrying what looked like emergency road flares crowded the cast-iron catwalk overlooking the main floor.

The dark interior of the store glowed eerily in the flares' wavering light. "It's weird," Tom said quietly. "Why don't they use flashlights?"

"Not enough illumination," Mitch whispered. "The store's electricity is still off, and they don't want to open the metal shutters or someone on the street might see them in here. They're obviously looking for the missing microprocessor."

As the brothers watched, the ninjas dragged boxes down from the shelves and ripped them open, spilling the contents to the floor far below. Appliances shattered on the linoleum, the debris piled high.

More flares sputtered on the ground floor. In the center of the room, the brothers spied Laura Ting. Her legs and wrists were tied to a metal folding chair with thick ropes. Her hair was disheveled and a bruise reddened the side of her face. The contents of her backpack were scattered on the floor around her feet. Two ninjas flanked the teenager, swords drawn. Laura's eyes were defiant as she gazed up at the giant who loomed over her.

"That must be that goon Maldeen," Tom whispered.

Roman Maldeen was the largest man Mitch had ever seen. At seven feet, he was a head taller than everyone else in the room. And he had shoulders so broad, Mitch wondered how he got through the door.

Tom observed the man too, noting that under his long overcoat, Roman Maldeen's physique seemed freakish. His head, crowned by a shock of black hair streaked with gray, seemed small for his massive body. Unlike the man's abnormally long legs, his thick arms seemed stunted, though unnaturally long fingers under black gloves made them appear normally proportioned—at least at first glance.

While they watched, Maldeen gripped Laura's head with those clawed fingers, lifting her pointed chin until their eyes met.

"You will give me what I want, child," he purred in a cruel tone. "My master is a giant of industry, a man with wealth and power. Look at me, girl. It isn't wise to challenge someone of *my* stature."

Laura smirked defiantly. "So you're big, and your boss is a *big shot*. So what. Big deal. I can't give you what I don't have." Laura's eyes flashed with anger, then narrowed with determination.

"I know you're lying, or you wouldn't be here," he cried. "If the processor wasn't hidden in this place, you'd be cowering in New Jersey with the rest of your family."

Laura struggled against her bonds. Roman Maldeen

threw back his head and laughed once, short and sharp. "No, my dear. You are not fooling me. You have the device and I want it. We know what your father's been working on. And we know he told you where he's hidden his secret. So it's no use lying, little one."

"What good is my father's invention to you and your boss?" Laura challenged.

Maldeen smirked. "Why should I reveal our plans to you?"

"Your *plans*," Laura scoffed. "I'll bet you don't even *understand* what my father invented."

Maldeen's fists clenched in fury. "You know nothing, little girl!" he shouted. "Julian Vane seeks to bring down the Internet. With your father's superfast processor in his possession, Vane will create computers powerful enough to swamp the world's technological infrastructure. All over the globe, servers will crash, fuse, or burn up. Then we will control cyberspace!"

From their hiding places, Tom and Mitch glanced at each other.

"This dude's crazy," Tom whispered.

"Nuts or not, Maldeen is going to hurt Laura even more if we don't stop him," replied Mitch.

"There are seven ninjas in there, and the giant guy, too," Tom pointed out. "Those are crummy odds."

To Tom's surprise, Mitch actually smiled.

"Something funny about that?" Tom asked.

"I just came up with a plan to thin their ranks considerably," said Mitch. "Unfortunately, it's risky, and I can't do it alone."

Now Tom was smiling too. "Guess it's a good thing you brought me along."

CHAPTER 14

Ten minutes later Tom and Mitch stepped out of the stairwell and into the flickering glow of the emergency flares. Mitch twirled the dagger over his head. Like a lasso, it swished through the air.

Tom wore thick rubber gloves, his hands gripping the bow. The string was stretched to the limit, a steel arrow ready to be loosed.

"Hey, you!" Mitch yelled.

The ninjas on the catwalk stopped their vandalism to stare in surprise. Seeing their reaction, Roman Maldeen whirled to face the brothers, his overcoat billowing like Dracula's cape.

"Release Laura now or he'll shoot," Mitch threatened in what he hoped was an intimidating tone.

Roman Maldeen sighed with exasperation. He eyed the brothers like two pesky flies he'd failed to smash with his swatter. "I was informed by my agents that we got rid of you two with your butler."

Mitch's eyes narrowed. "You missed, butthead."

"Free the girl or I'll loose this arrow," Tom warned.

Unfortunately, his threat didn't produce the response he was expecting. Behind his mask, one ninja snorted in derision. The others began to laugh and point.

"That's it!" Mitch cried to Tom. "Let 'em have it."

With a twang, the arrow launched. As it flew, a thin copper wire unspooled behind it. With a clang, the steel tip clattered across the catwalk. The copper wire connected with the iron, and the room exploded with blue sparks.

Ninjas howled, jolted as thousands of volts of electricity surged through the metal walkway. Jerking wildly, robes smoldering, they plunged over the rail to the floor, stunned into unconsciousness. Tiny fires, started by a thousand sparks, flared up around them.

The long wire that ran from the arrow, all the way back to the electrical power cables in the sewer, began to melt as more electricity than it could ever handle flowed through the copper thread.

It didn't matter. The wire had done its job. Five ninjas were down, and only two remained standing.

Tom dropped the bow and charged into the shop. He considered taking on one of the last ninjas—and avoiding the angry giant who now shouted commands to his underlings. At first he didn't want to tangle with Roman Maldeen if he didn't have to. But then he recalled what Mr. Chance had said right before the explosion: *"There is deception everywhere. Nothing is what it seems."*

Tom veered and rushed toward Maldeen. His attack was nothing fancy—more suited to a soccer game than the dojo. He simply dropped to the linoleum and slid right into the giant's legs, feet first.

Maldeen cried out as his legs flew out from under him. His coat fluttered as he struck the floor.

"You're not so tough after all," said Tom as he untangled himself from the man's voluminous clothing.

While Tom rained down blows on Maldeen's unprotected head, Mitch rushed to Laura's side. He ripped the double blade from his belt and spun it in his hand, slicing the ropes.

Laura jumped out of the chair. "Watch out!"

Mitch spied movement out of the corner of his eye and ducked. A sword arced over his head, shaving a blond lock.

Free now, Laura used a maneuver called the distracting hand to conceal her kick. While the ninja dodged her feint, a sudden blow to his kneecap sent him reeling. The man slammed against the wall behind the ruined counter. A framed dollar bill and several photographs and plaques were knocked to the floor.

Mitch picked up the folding chair and hurled it with all his might. The heavy metal frame slammed into the ninja and he went down for the count.

In the center of the floor, Tom grappled with Roman Maldeen. The man's long fingers raked his face as Maldeen groped for his throat. The giant was strong, but not skilled. Tangled together, the pair rolled over a patch of fire and the cloak ignited. As flames licked his body, Maldeen let out a high-pitched squeal and released Tom.

The fire quickly engulfed the giant. The last ninja standing sheathed his sword and ran to his master's rescue. While Maldeen howled, the ninja tore his clothes away and beat out the flames.

Mitch spied a glint of metal under the tall man's singed pants. More metal gleamed through holes in his black gloves.

Tom's eyes bugged. "This dude's not a giant at all! Maldeen's no bigger than we are. He's been walking on stilts! And his claws are fake too."

Flames began to rise all around them. The metal prosthetic devices fell away, and Maldeen's stubby arms and legs flailed wildly. So much smoke filled the store that the brothers soon lost sight of Maldeen and his crew.

Tom gripped his brother's arm. "We've got to get out of here," he gasped between coughs. "The store's going up in flames!"

Eyes stinging, Mitch was ready to go—then he realized Laura was nowhere to be found. Finally he spotted her through a break in the smoke. Laura was crouched behind the shattered counter, digging through pictures that had been knocked from the wall by the unconscious ninja on the floor next to her.

Mitch grabbed Laura's arm and headed for the stairs. But the emptied cardboard boxes were burning now, and flames blocked the stairs.

"We're trapped!" he cried.

Suddenly the building was rocked by a loud explosion.

"What the—?" Tom exclaimed.

Daylight filled the shop as the steel shutters dropped into the street.

"Look!" Laura yelled. "The metal shutters! The explosion knocked them out!"

"Through the window, quick," commanded Tom.

Mitch pulled Laura to the window, then jumped through to the street. Laura stumbled, and Mitch lifted her through the opening. He noticed she was clutching a framed photograph to her chest.

Blackened by smoke, the trio stumbled across Mott Street. Coughing, they collapsed in a heap on the sidewalk. Noonday shoppers were now fleeing the smoke and flames that licked the walls of Ting Microsystems.

"Where did that explosion come from?" Tom wondered. "Laura, was your dad stockpiling nitro or something?"

"No way," she said.

"Weird," said Mitch. "Something like a gas main would have taken out the whole building. That explosion seemed surgical, like it was targeted to take out the shutters alone, and only the shutters."

Laura's face looked pale under the black smudges. But to Tom and Mitch's surprise, she began to laugh.

"Why are you so happy?" Tom asked.

"Because of this," she whispered, holding up a

photograph of herself with the first prize trophy from last year's Citywide Science Fair.

As she pointed to the broken frame and cracked glass, Tom and Mitch saw that a transparent Mylar envelope had been tucked between the photo and the frame. The bag contained the prototype processor, along with a thumb drive containing the schematics to manufacture it.

As Laura laughed, a single tear cut a trail through the grime on her cheek. "My father really *did* hide the secret close to his heart, just like he said."

CHAPTER 15

It was midafternoon when the trio finally returned to Tom and Mitch's brownstone. On First Avenue, the car wreckage had been cleared. Only scorched concrete remained to remind the brothers of their next challenge.

They'd solved Laura Ting's mystery, but now they had another. Was Mr. Chance dead or alive? Was he in the car when it exploded? Or had he gotten out of the car in time to slip away? What exactly had happened during that terrible explosion?

"I feel responsible for what happened to Mr. Chance," Laura confessed. "I deceived you both. Tricked you into helping me. That note I left—"

"We know," Mitch replied. "Why would you leave a note telling us where you went if you didn't really want us to follow you, right?"

"I knew you were keeping things from me, and I

didn't know why," Laura explained. "But I figured if you came to find me, then I'd know you really wanted to help, and that I could trust you. If not, then it didn't matter anyway."

"Don't feel guilty," Tom said. "Mr. Chance knew your note was a ruse, even before we did. He tried to tell us too . . . in his own way."

Tom reached into his pocket for the key. But before he slipped it into the lock, the door opened. The brothers gasped when they saw a ghost in the doorway.

"There you are, young sirs—and quite the mess, too," Mr. Chance declared.

"Mr. Chance! You *are* alive!" Mitch cried. The brothers rushed the man and threw their arms around him.

"My, my," Mr. Chance said. "What a display!"

Tom laughed. "I really should have known. The Chance Man said it himself: 'Nothing is what it seems.'"

"Yeah," said Mitch. "And don't forget that other pearl of wisdom: 'In times of conflict, even your allies will deceive you.'"

Mr. Chance frowned. "I am sorry I had to fool you both," he said. "I felt it necessary to provide cover for your operation. If the ninjas believed you were both dead, I surmised they might let their guard down. I noticed assassins lying in wait on the roof across the street, so I gave them the perfect target of opportunity."

"You sure fooled us," Mitch said, smoothing his singed hair. "But how did you survive the bomb?"

"Actually, it was a handheld missile," Mr. Chance replied. "And I didn't survive, for I was never in the car."

Mitch laughed again when the butler showed them a tiny remote-control unit. "I *was* driving, young sirs—from the comfort of my bedroom window upstairs."

Mr. Chance ushered them in, closed the door. "You smell like a fire sale. I think you should wash up. Dinner will be served in an hour. The guest room is prepared to receive Ms. Ting as well."

Next to the stairs, Tom and Mitch stopped dead when they saw a bundle on the ground.

"What's C4?" Tom asked, reading the label.

"A highly explosive substance," replied Mitch with a raised eyebrow. "Powerful enough to blow *steel shutters* off a building." He shifted his gaze to Mr. Chance. "You followed us again, didn't you? What is this, some kind of initiation? Were you testing how we'd do on our own?"

Before Mr. Chance could answer, Laura Ting threw

her arms around the man's neck. "Thank you, sir!" she cried. "Thank you for saving us all."

"Wait a minute," Tom protested. "How come he gets the hug? We had a little something to do with your rescue too."

"And I am proud to say you both did very well," Mr. Chance concluded. "Very well indeed."

Mitch grinned and pretended to polish his fingernails on his chest. "Actually, it wasn't that hard."

"There is an old Japanese proverb," Mr. Chance went on. "*Beginning is easy. Continuing is hard.*"

"You mean it isn't over?" asked Laura.

Mr. Chance turned toward a credenza in the hall. "Before I forget, this package was delivered while you were gone. Though it was addressed to you, I took the liberty of opening it."

He handed them a thick folder. Inside, Mitch and Tom found first-class airplane tickets and passports.

"We're going to Japan?" Tom cried.

Mr. Chance nodded. "Certain sources suggest that your fathers' disappearances may be tied to Julian Vane. I also have it on good authority that he's in Japan as we speak, and I can guarantee you he isn't there on vacation. I think it is time we fill in some of the missing pieces to this puzzle, and put an end to Mr. Vane's abductions once and for all."

"Hey," Tom cried. "There are *four* tickets here! Four passports, too."

Chance nodded. "One for each of you, one for me— and one for Ms. Ting, of course."

Tom's jaw dropped. "You mean—"

Chance nodded. "Yes. Laura is already a member, should she choose to accept her fate."

Laura blinked. "A member? Of what?"

Mitch placed an arm around Laura's shoulder.

"Remember last night, when Tom brought up the subject of ronin?"

"Yeah, sure," Laura said. "But like I told you already, I don't watch violent films."

Mitch smiled. "We actually had something else in mind. . . ."

DON'T MISS THE NEXT
47 R.O.N.I.N. ADVENTURE:

EPISODE 2 THE SHOWDOWN

Here's a sneak peek. . . .

"I'm here again," Tom whispered, *"back on the island. . . ."*

He could smell the sea air and feel the high winds, whipping around the lone mountaintop. The symbol of R.O.N.I.N. loomed over him, a majestic jade dragon with glowing emeralds for eyes, the mysterious cave entrance hidden behind it.

Then Tom heard the sound of insistent beating; it was coming from helicopter blades. Like hungry raptors, the black choppers swarmed the island. Circling the mountain, they swooped closer and closer with each new pass.

Finally one of the choppers bucked, and a missile arrowed toward him, a white plume painting its path through the night. Tom gasped as the rocket slammed the side of the mountain. The fiery explosion shook rocks loose and sent them tumbling down the sheer cliffs.

A moment later he was deep inside the cave again, within the vast jade chamber.

"Oh no, the Scroll!" called a voice from the cave entrance. The Dragon's voice!

Then the voice of the Dragon spoke again.

"Thomas . . . you must save them! You and your brother! Do you understand?"

Men in black battle suits surged past the jade dragon and into the cave, machine guns raised.

侍

"NO! Save what?"

Tom's own cry woke him and brought Mitch and Mr. Chance racing to his side.

"Dude, what's wrong?" cried Mitch.

"It's the scroll! I think someone's trying to take it!"

DYLAN SPROUSE AND COLE SPROUSE ARE TWO OF HOLLYWOOD'S MOST EMINENT RISING STARS.

Dylan and Cole were born in Arezzo, Italy, and currently reside in Los Angeles, California. Named for the jazz singer and pianist Nat King Cole, Cole's list of favorites includes math, the color blue, and animals. He also enjoys video games and all types of sports, including motocross, snowboarding, and surfing. Dylan, named after the poet Dylan Thomas, is very close to his brother and also has a great love of animals and video games. He enjoys science, the Los Angeles Lakers, and the color orange. He's a sports enthusiast and especially loves motocross, snowboarding, surfing, and basketball.

Cole and Dylan made their acting debuts on the big screen in *Big Daddy*, opposite Adam Sandler. Both also starred in *The Astronaut's Wife*, *Master of Disguise*, and *Eight Crazy Nights*. On television Cole and Dylan established themselves in the critically acclaimed ABC comedy series *Grace Under Fire* and eventually went on to star in NBC's *Friends* as David Schwimmer's son, Ben Geller.

Dylan and Cole currently star as the introspective Cody Martin and the mischievous Zack Martin, respectively, in the Disney Channel's amazingly successful sitcom *The Suite Life of Zack and Cody*, playing separate roles for the first time. Ranked number one in its time slot against all basic cable shows, *The Suite Life* is now one of the Disney Channel's top shows and is rapidly gaining worldwide success.

In September 2005 the Sprouses partnered with Dualstar Entertainment Group to launch the *Sprouse Bros.* brand, the only young men's lifestyle brand designed by boys for boys. The brand includes *Sprouse Bros. 47 R.O.N.I.N.*, an apparel collection, an online fan club, mobile content, a DVD series in development, and lots more in the works!